D1552566

A THOUSAND BRIDGES

A THOUSAND BRIDGES

A Novel

Michael McKinney

Walker and Company
New York

F
M

All the characters and events portrayed in this work are fictitious.

First published in the United States of America in 1992 by Walker Publishing Company, Inc.

Published simultaneously in Canada by Thomas Allen & Son Canada, Limited, Markham, Ontario.

Library of Congress Cataloging-in-Publication Data
McKinney, Michael.
A thousand bridges : a novel / Michael McKinney.
p.   cm.
ISBN 0-8027-1223-1
I. Title.
PS3563.C3817T4   1992
813'.54—dc20   92-15737
CIP

Printed in the United States of America

2 4 6 8 10 9 7 5 3 1

To Margaret. First,
and always.
And to my son, Grif,
who admonished me
to finish what I
start.

Acknowledgments

Thanks to Sherri Hicks-Barnes for the proofreading and those first words of encouragment. To Pam Sutton and Mike Stone for the support and friendship. Thanks to Gloria and Kenneth Pipkin, for so much help and conversation.
And to my sister, Pat, for believing in me.

A THOUSAND BRIDGES

ONE

It was too damned hot to work, so Sheevers and I had sat on the sofa, close but not touching. She had been drinking from a large glass of iced tea, making little movements with her wrist that caused the ice cubes to swirl and tinkle, then opened the first two buttons on her blouse and rubbed the moist glass across her chest. I remember she handed it to me and when I put my lips on the rim I could taste her perfume. I made a face and she laughed, lifted the glass from my fingers, and stood up. "I'll get us a refill," she said, and I watched her until she disappeared through the doorway to the small kitchen.

The morning paper lay unopened on the coffee table and I leaned forward with a groan, lifted it, and fell back against the cushions. We'd had a long night, partly working but mostly celebrating. Patty Sheevers was my new silent partner in the private-investigations business I'd been building for almost three years in Palmetto Bay, Florida. It would still be called McDonald Clay Investigations, but now we were together at work as well as at home. She thought the two of us would be like the Thin Man, and I was beginning to believe it, too.

A breeze slipped through the screen door as I unfolded my newspaper, and a cloud obscured the sun. The air felt cooler and I wished for rain. I heard Sheevers singing in the other room. The headlines told, for a second straight day, about a recent multiple murder at a local swimming hole. The press and police were calling it the Limestone Creek Murders.

"Something's not right here," I said, looking at the color photograph of the scene. Sheevers sat on the coffee table, folded the paper down, and looked at the picture, grinning.

"How can you say that?" she asked. "It looks like an ordinary murder to me."

It didn't look right. I should have examined it more thoroughly, taken more interest, but we were so wrapped up in our first case

[1]

together, so pleased with the confidence the state's attorney had shown in hiring us to investigate Tommy Lovett, that it didn't seem important. And it wasn't, at the time.

Sheevers handed over a full glass of tea and made off with the Local/State section of the paper. This was her town. She sat across from me in the chair, stretched out her legs, and propped her bare feet up on the coffee table. I sipped my tea. "Are we going to get any work done today, Mac?" she said when she finished reading. I glanced around at the notes and copies of articles that overflowed my desk and spread like the Andes across the carpet, past Sheevers's lighted aquarium to the corner of the sofa.

"Yeah," I said reluctantly, not really wanting to get into the case of Tommy Lovett on such a hot day. The state's attorney had hired us, off the record, to gather enough evidence on Lovett to send him away forever, and Sheevers wanted nothing short of that. I didn't know that much about him when I'd started the investigation, except that he owned a large pool hall downtown called Tommy's and hung around with some very important people. It didn't take long to find out how powerful he was. We hadn't been on the case a week when word got to him that I was checking him out. When I drove down to my office the next day, I found all my filing cabinets turned over in the middle of the floor and the files flung from wall to wall. That is, all except the ones on Tommy Lovett. They were gone. From that day on we kept duplicates of his case at home, and that's where we began to work each day.

Tommy Lovett personally hired the young girls who racked the balls at his pool hall. Through the years he had selected some of these girls, usually around sixteen years old, to discreetly "entertain" visiting dignitaries at the locally famous Sunset Hotel downtown. The ornate heart of Palmetto Bay for almost a hundred years, the Sunset was a pinnacle of old money and power, the register a roster of legends from around the Florida Panhandle. Sports heroes and politicians, men whose names were the names of streets and hospitals and schools— and Patty hated them all.

I'd met her two years before at my lawyer's office out on the beach. She'd been sitting beside him on a small deck that faced the water, her blond hair whipping around in the erratic wind. She looked up at me when I reached the table, and pulled the twisted golden strands from her eyes. She smiled. Mark introduced us politely, but I don't think he wanted me to stay. I've never been able to take a hint. She and I started talking about politics and religion and life and death, and the next

[2]

thing I knew Mark Thornton had gone inside, and the next thing I knew, Patty Sheevers and I were living together and I was madly in love.

She had been trying to sell me on the idea of her being my partner since we met, but until this thing with Tommy Lovett my business hadn't exactly been lucrative. It paid the bills and, every once in a while, left us with enough money at the end of the month to go out for dinner. Her job kept us afloat. The job with the state's attorney was our turning point, not only because the money was good, but it was too much work for one person to handle. Finally one morning, after months of preparation, we decided there was enough information to take to Tallahassee. That night Sheevers and I sat in bed under a single sheet that billowed like a sail each time the oscillating fan swept by, whispering how the old names in town were going to be nailed like hides to a barn wall and cured by the state's attorney. Her eyes flashed excitement in the yellow glow of the hall light, and as she waved her arms, her small, perfect breasts swayed, hypnotizing me like a snake in a basket.

I spent the next day in town wrapping up the case by interviewing frightened teenage girls and their angry parents. None of us wanted to be there, and because Tommy's men had been everywhere before me, it turned out to be a waste of time. I hated working downtown. My first decent lungful of air came as I was headed home, turning past the marina toward the north side. Shrimp boats made their way back to the docks under swirling clouds of seagulls, shimmering white confetti that dipped and dove for scraps in the wake of the boats. Red and green lights winked along the dark channel of the bay, and pink street lamps flickered to life on the far shore. A salt breeze rattled palm fronds outside my open window as I waited at the intersection for a break in traffic. I heard a man shout, "Hey, asshole!" and I turned my head to see if he was talking to me. I'd answered to that name before. A white Lincoln Continental had eased up alongside, and I saw Tommy Lovett grinning at me from the back seat. He winked.

"You think you're gonna get me busted, ace?" he shouted across the space between us. He looked freshly scrubbed and pampered, black hair wet and brushed back against his narrow head. A beautiful young woman sitting beside him laughed and shook her head, her butter-scotch curls melting over the shoulders of a milk-white dress. Lovett snorted, "Jesus, you're a stupid fucker." He shook his head and tapped the driver on the arm. His car cut in front of mine and darted into traffic while I sat there trying to think of something witty to say. A

[3]

dozen things came to mind as I drove home. The French have a word for it, something to do with the "wit of the staircase."

I parked beside Sheevers's car and rolled my window closed, suddenly tired and irritable. I sat with the door open for a few seconds, exhaled, and watched dusk capture the sky. Her sunshade had fallen across the steering wheel, and I pushed it back up. The morning sun would be toasting that windshield long before we were ready to leave for Tallahassee. We had a lot of finishing up yet to do on the case, and work wasn't on the agenda for the evening. There were two bottles of cheap wine sharing the refrigerator with a crab salad and a bowl of boiled shrimp, so I shook off the mood as I walked across the yard. I stepped onto my small porch, opened the screen door, and stepped inside, loosening a new tie Sheevers had insisted I wear to the day's interviews. She said it would give me an aura of authority, but it hadn't helped. I tapped on the open door to let her know I was home and smelled tea brewing on the stove.

"Hello?" I called out as I walked into the kitchen, but she wasn't there. I turned off the burner and picked up the teapot. She'd let the water steam out, and the bottom of the pot was glowing red. It wasn't the first time that had happened, but it was usually I who did it. I put it down and walked back into the living room, past my cluttered desk to the lighted aquarium, glancing at her bright, quick tropical fish as I stepped into the hall. The bedroom lamp was out, but a seam of white light leaked from the closed bathroom door. I turned the knob and pushed, but she was holding it closed, so I laughed, put a shoulder into it, and shoved hard enough to win entrance. I jumped sideways through the opening before she could shut it, and my black dress shoes slipped in a viscous puddle of darkening blood. Sheevers lay on the bathroom floor with her blouse ripped open, her hands tied behind her back. She was bleeding from so many knife wounds that a whole box of Kleenex couldn't stop them all, and even as I crawled around on the sticky, stinking floor begging to a silent God, I knew she was dead.

My screaming roused the neighbors from supper, and they called the police. Someone found a ski mask and a knife in the jasmine beside the screened porch, and Sheevers's watch on the lawn. Sheriff Hall stood in my doorway and said, "She musta' interrupted a burglar," and someone said, "Yeah."

"Goddamn you!" I shouted at them, and when the sheriff nodded toward me they put me in cuffs and dragged me to the patrol car, pushing my neighbors off the sidewalk as they folded me into the back seat.

[4]

"Why?" a neighbor asked.

"We have to make sure it wasn't him," a deputy said as I sat in the back seat of the police car and slammed my body against the inside of the door. "He's acting strange."

I was placed in isolation; a small, soundproofed cell with a solid, seamless door. For three days they kept me in that tiny room with no radio, no visitors, no sounds but my own. There was one bright, bare light bulb shielded with wire, set in the ceiling out of my reach. Three days with one memory. Three days of thinking that I should have known something was going to happen.

That was five years ago and I'd been ambitious, and had a good reputation. It's not that I have a bad reputation now. The fact is, I have no reputation. I've sold out so many times and for so many reasons that I'm like the white boxer brought in to fill the card, not because he's a contender, but because he's such a good bleeder. I make the other guy look good. I'm not ashamed of it. The bleeder gets paid after the fight, too, he just never gets to wear the belt. Besides, this is a small city and I like living here. I have memories in Palmetto Bay.

It didn't take long to go downhill from the jail cell. When they let me out it was like a metamorphosis. The butterfly that spread its wings in the blazing sun was as empty as the cell he'd just left. Vacant. When people touched me and said, "I'm sorry," I cried.

They had buried her that morning and let me out in the afternoon. Somebody drove me home and a policeman let me in. I ran to the bathroom and it was cleaner than we'd ever kept it. It smelled like ammonia and soap. There wasn't even a hair in the sink to show where Sheevers had been. I ripped the medicine cabinet from the wall and the front door clicked open, the policeman peeked inside, and the door closed again. The house had been carelessly ransacked and our things were everywhere. The vein in my temple pounded so fiercely, it was like being slapped. I yanked the manila envelope from my jacket and tore it open, pulling the keys and wallet from a pile of loose articles the police had collected from my pockets.

I let myself out and didn't acknowledge the cop. My car had been rifled and the back seat was popped up where they left it after their search. I didn't bother straightening any of it out, just cranked up and aimed the car toward the cemetery.

It wasn't hard to find her grave. Like I said, this place is big enough to be called a city, but not big enough to get lost in. Not so big that a freshly dug grave doesn't stand out in a flat, ten-acre field of manicured grass and low markers and a giant statue of a resting Jesus. There she was, covered with dirt for eternity, and all I could do was stand around looking goofy with tears pouring down my cheeks, blinking like mad to see the little plastic marker pushed into the ground. Someone with poor handwriting had scrawled her name on the marker with a grease pencil: "Patricia Sheevers."

I drove away dangerously. Alert, gracious drivers made room for me as I wheeled from the somber gates and back onto the road, oblivious to the world. I stopped at a convenience store and bought a copy of the day's newspaper, where hers was still a front-page story, but on the lower right side. It had surely occupied a more prominent position the previous two days.

The article mentioned she was a local woman and her parents were "distraught." I was said to have been a "possible suspect" but was being released for lack of evidence. The state's attorney couldn't be reached for comment. The sheriff did say the crime rate in our area was up and that drugs made "ordinary kids" do things like this, though there were no leads. He said they'd probably never know.

As I sat in my car reading the article, I thought I was experiencing an eclipse of the sun. There, just before three o'clock on an early-September afternoon, a darkness fell on me layer by layer until I had the newspaper just inches from my face, trying to read it. I looked up, shocked, and the world around me was darker than midnight. I could see shapes and movements and hear muffled noises, but I couldn't tell where I was and it scared the hell out of me. I pushed the paper away and fumbled for the key, slamming my knuckles into the dash as I felt a blind panic numbing me. I looked around helplessly in the dark but saw no one there, nowhere to turn.

Suddenly, fiercely, a terror shook me and I scratched at the door, opening it and pushing it away from me as I bent out and began throwing up in the small parking lot. My fingers gripped the wheel and the seat as I leaned out, knifing pains tearing at my stomach as I heaved my insides onto the concrete. It finally stopped, and as I hung from the car I heard someone say, "Jesus Christ!" People began pulling away from the store.

I heard a man shouting and I looked up, wiping my face on my sleeve. An older man in a white shirt and a little blue vest had pushed open the market door and held it as he stood on the sidewalk. "Get the hell out of here!" he almost screamed at me as his lost business hurriedly cranked their cars and raced from the store. I squinted at him in the direct sunlight, now brilliant again. I straightened up, still aware of the pains in my stomach, and closed the door. When I finally got my car started I backed out, not looking at him as I drove away.

That's when two things hit me. The first was I couldn't get mad at anyone. I was no longer capable of anger, my emotions neutered in the isolated jail cell. After that day, any time anything bad happened or someone I didn't like did something I didn't like, I simply felt empty and blank, like a man with a concussion trying to remember how he got cracked on the head. It just wasn't there.

The second thing was the similarity between Sheevers's death and the Limestone Creek Murders. Not that they were connected, but the coverage was the same. Both stories were simply reported and settled on the spot. Not one detective on the force said, "It couldn't have happened that way," or, in the Limestone Creek case, "What the hell was a black hustler like Renaldo Tippit doing up in redneck country at night on a three-wheeler?" No reporter questioned his sources, no outside agency stepped in to snoop around. The stories were just filed as stated, nothing more. Business as usual.

That's what bothered me the day Sheevers and I read the story about the three killings at Limestone Creek. It just wasn't right for a crime to come fully solved right from the factory. There were always loose ends and surprises, even in open-and-shut cases. I knew Patty's murder was doctored and I knew why, but the other one bugged me. It looked simple enough—a drug deal gone bad. A forty-year-old man and a teenage boy and girl were shot to death at a remote creek in the far end of the county during a drug buy. The dealer, well known to the local police for his drug activity, raced away from the scene on a three-wheeled all-terrain vehicle and turned onto the two-lane county black-top directly in the path of an eighteen-wheeler driven by a man from Alabama. There was very little left of Renaldo or his motorcycle. That was the story.

But it wasn't the truth. It couldn't have been. I knew Renaldo and he wasn't such a bad guy, as drug pushers go. He operated almost exclusively from an area of town known as the "Supermarket." It was a much-publicized part of the blighted core of Palmetto Bay's "black side" of town, and even though more dope was sold out of beach condos in a weekend than the Supermarket moved in a month, it was what people pictured in their minds when drug deals were mentioned in the press.

I knew Renaldo Tippit because we met so often in the courthouse. I was always bumming cigarettes from him. One day he laughed and told me he was going to get me started selling dope for him so I could buy my own "damned smokes." He was one of the two people who shamed me into quitting the habit, Sheevers being the other. I can't say that I really liked him, but I can't really say I like most people I meet.

The thing is, like most blacks in the county, Renaldo knew his boundaries. He was aware of "the way things were." Not that this is peculiar to the South. The average blacks who worked hard and raised their families and tried to achieve the American Dream winced when they passed the Supermarket and wished Renaldo and company would go elsewhere, but knew there was nowhere else to go. Like the tourist-trap Indians surrounded by Chinese blankets along the roadside, inner-city blacks were expected to put on a show. That's why the image of Renaldo Tippit making a dope deal in the woods on an ATV three-wheeler should have set off alarms all along the law-enforcement ladder. The fact that it didn't was what made my bell ring, but I never had a bridge to use to solve the puzzle. And now, after five years, there wasn't enough left of me that still wanted to try.

I had only one friend who survived my abuses during that time. Mark Thornton was not only brilliant and handsome, but a shoo-in to become a partner in the law firm of Barrett, Barrett and Finch. Because of him I kept my home. Because of him food appeared in my refrigerator and my clothes were returned clean from the laundry. He made a present of electricity and running water. We'd met during one of my divorce cases, and after a few months of working together, were surprised to find we liked each other. Nothing complex, we just laughed at each other's jokes and became friends. He never once mentioned the day I stepped in between him and Patty Sheevers, but I know he loved her.

I lost the desire to be a detective after Sheevers's death, but I couldn't get other work, either. The people of Palmetto Bay didn't encourage me to stay, but I couldn't leave. Patty was still there, alive in my house, holding my hand and talking to me in the darkness as I searched for the nerve to join her. I failed in that just as I'd failed to find the ones who had killed her.

I became an errand boy mostly, and my main employer was Bob Birk, a businessman turning politician. He owned a lot of the beach-front property, along with a few businesses, the school board, and the sheriff's department. Of course, he controlled the last two only because of a deep-seated desire to help the people of Palmetto Bay. It was rumored that Birk was considering a run for governor. His succeeding wasn't beyond the realm of possibility.

I had pulled myself back up in the last couple of years, but not too far. I had no intention of having my own business again, I just wanted to be invisible. But at about the time I thought I was going to pull it off, I met an angry, frightened woman who had nothing left but defiance. And defiance is my favorite emotion.

TWO

It wasn't a coincidence, a matter of throwing darts at the yellow pages. She specifically wanted me. I don't really have an office anymore, things being the way they are; I just work out of the house. And even that's not necessary—a phone booth would do. Outside of an occasional Jehovah's Witness or a kids' paper drive, nobody usually rings my doorbell. I was cooking dinner and almost dropped the pan when I heard it. Looking every bit a real detective, a dish towel over my shoulder and a bottle of soy sauce in my hand, I opened the door. The first thing she did was laugh—a real laugh, with humor in it.

"I'm impressed," she said.

Screen doors are like the fountain of youth. They soften reality and remove the rough edges of age and life, and if the wealthy knew that, poor people would be priced out of the screen-door market. She looked softly pretty through the screen, but, to my surprise, she looked the same when I opened the door and she stepped inside. She was in her middle thirties, I guessed, with thick, dark-brown hair and bright green eyes. Her hair didn't signal her age, but was styled fresh and loose.

She looked at me as though she knew me, but there's no way I'd have forgotten that face. Her eyes were spaced a little too far apart, but that only heightened the effect her smile created. I tried to act as if this sort of thing happened all the time.

"What can I do for you?" I said.

"I need a detective."

"I can recommend a few."

"I want you," she said.

We were still standing inside the front door, my small screened porch at her back. Even though she looked around the living room, I wasn't about to invite her in. I hoped she'd notice I was being rude, but she seemed comfortable.

"New in town?" I asked.

"I haven't been here in a long time. But I was raised here."

"I thought maybe you were a stranger." I was patient with her. "You see, I'm not really a detective."

"That's not what I heard," she said softly.

"What?"

"Patty Sheevers used to tell me you could do anything." Her eyes never left mine. It's strange, I really meant to say something, but it was as though the world stopped in its tracks. I was aware of her in front of me and I knew I wasn't doing what I should, but it had been a long time since anyone had mentioned Sheevers and I froze. She took my arm and led me to my oversize chair, tugging until I took a seat. She sat on the sofa and looked at me across the coffee table.

"My name is Katherine Furay," she said. "Patty and I grew up together. You probably don't remember me—we never met—but Patty used to come to my house when you were away."

Sheevers did things like that. She'd say, "I'm not going to stay in this house by myself with you gone," and when I returned, there would be a phone number paper-clipped to the screen door. Sometimes just a note saying, 'I'll be home Wednesday.'

I still couldn't think of anything to say, so I just sat there sweating. She waited, until finally, I leaned forward and said, "Patty's dead."

"I know." It was a whisper. She took the towel from my shoulder and wiped my face. I felt really stupid. "I read about it in Las Vegas," she said, rising from the sofa. She brushed the pleated, chocolate-colored skirt across her knees, a fascinating assortment of curves and angles as she walked out of my line of sight. "But I've sort of been in hiding for the last few years. I couldn't come to the funeral."

"That's okay," I said, "A lot of us missed it."

She stopped moving somewhere behind me, then I heard her footsteps, heard her stop behind my chair. "You weren't there?"

I found the words. "The police didn't let me out until it was over. Her father sent word later that if he ever saw me he'd kill me. He dared me to say I was sorry. Some people think I did it."

"My God," she said, putting her hands on my shoulders. "No one has ever told you how much Patty loved you?"

"Please," I said.

"You were her knight," Katherine Furay said. "I used to get jealous when she talked about you."

I pulled away from her and stood up, spinning around to face her. "What do you want?" I said, "And why do you keep touching me?"

[11]

My bitterness stung her, and I was immediately sorry. She flinched and drew away from me, and I wondered how many times she had been knocked around. As self-assured as she'd seemed a minute ago, I never would have believed it, but I watched her confidence crash down, silent as a house of cards. One delicate hand drew up, slender fingers circling the other wrist.

"These are the best clothes I have," she said, and I must have looked puzzled. "I'm trying to find a place to start. I keep touching you because you're my only link to everything here, and right now that's all I have. Patty used to tell me how good you were and what a great detective you were, and I guess I've built you up a little larger than life. I'm sorry."

"Kate!" I said it too loud. "You're Kate!" She looked at the door, and I thought she was going to make a run for it. "That's what Sheevers called you. She'd say, 'I'm going to Kate's.' "

"That's me," she said, gaining a little composure.

"You had a daughter."

"I still do," she said, and there was fear in her eyes. "Listen, I'm screwing this all up. It's just that I've pretended to have this conversation for so long, and you're not saying the things I imagined you saying. Not at all."

"Sorry." She laughed again, only a little, but it was like absolution. "I want to be honest with you, Kate, but you'll have to believe me." I closed the door and sat back down. She returned to the sofa but stayed on her feet. I leaned against the cushions. "Maybe I used to be both those things—good, and a good detective. But I'm not now, not anymore. This isn't bullshit. I'm not wallowing here but I'm completely and totally serious. I work for the men Sheevers and I despised—hell, I work for anybody, but not doing detective work." She looked nervous, and she sat down on the sofa's rounded edge.

"You can't have big dreams and be a detective in this town. Like most everything else around here, it pays something like minimum wage and there's not a great deal of world-class detecting to do anyhow. If that's not enough, I've lost the touch. Not to mention the desire. I simply file papers and run errands, and when they need someone to back up a story, they call me." I shrugged. "That's it."

We sat in a silence broken only by the gentle bubbling of the aquarium, and when I looked down at my hands I realized I was still holding the bottle of soy sauce. I leaned over and placed it on the coffee table. A car passed by and its tires hissed at the road. Part of me wanted her to stay and talk, but a larger part wanted her to leave. She stood up, and I didn't look at her. She walked away but, once again, she missed the door. Memories of Sheevers were like broken glass to me, and most nights I sat up late, thinking of her. I saved that for me alone, however, and right now I had an intruder in my life. I tried to ignore her.

"There aren't any fish in here," she said, and I knew she had reached the aquarium.

"I know."

"Why not?"

"They died."

"When?" She was so damned curious.

"I don't know," I said. "A couple of years ago, maybe. I can't remember."

"So why do you still keep it going like this?"

I stood up and turned to her, stuffing my hands into my pockets. She was facing away from me, looking into the tank, her fingers touching the water. She didn't seem to have a bad side, and I was glad she didn't know I was ogling.

"I'm beginning to see a pattern," I said. She didn't say anything. "You're not going to leave until you tell me why you came here, are you?"

She still didn't say anything. I thought about my food, cold on the stove. I thought about Patty Sheevers, and I would until I could get rid of Katherine Furay. I'd still think about her, but this was different somehow.

"Are you religious, Mac?"

"I'm a Hereditarian," I said. "I believe if your parents went to Heaven when they died, you will, too." Silence again. She was getting on my nerves. But then, in the stillness of an encroaching dusk, I heard her crying. It was so quiet, such a terribly personal thing, that I was embarrassed for her. The food could wait, and I felt like an ass. I had been trying so hard to remain aloof that I was acting like a jerk, and to make matters worse, I couldn't remember how not to be one.

I crossed the room and placed my right hand on her back. It seemed I'd said more than enough already, so I kept my mouth shut. She was soft and warm, and under my palm I could feel the ripples of captured air move through her as she fought the tears. "I want to believe in God," she said. "It was easy when I was a little girl, but it's so hard now." She leaned back against my hand and hung her head, her brow resting on the cool glass of the tank. When she continued, her voice was so low and toneless I could tell it was part of the speech she'd practiced.

[13]

"When my daughter was fourteen years old, she was raped by Bob Birk at the Sunset Hotel, but she didn't tell me until she found out she was pregnant. I put a gun in my purse and went to his office to kill him, and he laughed at me." Her tears were gone, replaced by a calm, lived-in kind of hatred. "He said he wasn't surprised Candy was pregnant, since it was common knowledge that I was fifteen when I had her. He said whoring seemed to run in the family, then he took the gun away and slapped me. He told me to go home and he'd take care of Candace's 'problem.' " Katherine Furay turned to me and her face was like polished stone. "Goddamn it, Mac, he raped my little girl and I let him send her to get an abortion. She came home with an envelope that had five thousand dollars in it, and a note saying I should get Candy out of town and if we ever came back he'd have her taken away from me. And he could've done it."

This last was said with an aching resignation made worse because I knew she was right. We stood just inches apart in a house that was getting very dark, and the air was thick and warm. Her eyes were black slits with fire inside and her wide mouth was a thin line, and, right in the middle of this, my stomach made a noise you could only imitate by burping into a slide whistle.

Her eyes popped open, and I was overwhelmed by that horrible feeling you get when you not only notice your fly is open but realize that it has been for some time. She saved me by laughing so hard that she sloshed water out of my aquarium. The laughter had reached hysterical proportions by the time she clutched my sleeve and fell against me, and all my feelings of humiliation were dwarfed by a sudden and powerful sexual desire. It caught me by surprise, and I almost wrapped my arms around her.

I was confused and shaken, afraid to speak when she finally caught her breath. She straightened up, sucked in a chuckle, and brushed past me, shooting sparks only I could see. I didn't move. To say my sexual drive had been nothing to write home about would be like saying Hitler had been impetuous. I hurriedly tried to sort my thoughts into some proper order when she said, "I think I'd better go now."

"Why?" I said, too fast.

"Because," she said, "I'm trying to dump five years of hate on you in one breath, and you don't even know me; I'm really very sorry, but I'm so angry and scared, and I'm afraid that all you'll see is a madwoman grasping for an anchor.

"I put on the best clothes I have to come see you, because I wanted

[14]

you to listen to me and because I don't know where else to go." The hysteria was returning, but this time there was no laughter.

"Candace tried to kill herself a couple of months ago, and she almost made it. God, I thought we'd gotten over everything and it had been a long time since her last depression. She was dating a guy in Las Vegas this winter, and he dumped her.

"Candy's really messed up, Mac," she said. "And I always thought it was the abortion. She was obsessed with death and horribly gruesome things, and after she . . . did what she did, I took her to a therapist.

"Wait a minute!" She shook her head. "Here I go again!"

She turned slightly and slipped her hand into a purse I hadn't even noticed, great detective that I am. She pulled out a pen and pad and flipped open the red leather cover. "I'm going to leave you my phone number in Las Vegas. If you want to help me, if you want to talk—"

"Hold on!" I snapped up the bait like a hungry fish. "You're not about to dump a story like that on me and walk out the door! Now, sit down and wait until I warm up some food. I'm sure there's still more than one plate in the house."

I went from room to room and turned on almost every light in a strange kind of exorcism, but she didn't ask and I didn't elaborate. She followed me into the kitchen and sat at the small oak table while I tried to salvage the meal. We ate a late supper of limp stir-fry, but the wine was okay and we were both hungry enough to forgive the little sins of the cook.

We didn't talk much as we ate. She was too tired and I was too scared, but by the second glass of wine I had relaxed and sorted things out. The way I had it figured, it was her closeness to Sheevers and not her sensuality that had me on the ropes. I was transferring my love for Patty to her closest friend. The sobering fact that her vulnerability added to my lust threw on just enough guilt for a full load, and I forged an explanation I could live with.

I made a fresh pot of coffee and cleaned the dishes as it perked. Katherine went to freshen up, and when I glanced up from the two filled cups, she was leaning in the doorless arch, watching me. It had been a long time since anyone had looked at me that way.

"These aren't exactly office hours," I said. "But I want you to tell me the rest. To be honest, I still don't know why you need a detective. I think a lawyer would do you more good, especially with the rumors that our Mister Birk is going to run for governor on the ultraright conservative ticket; you know, antiabortion and all that?" "Teaser"

[15]

billboards had been showing up along the interstate as well as some of the more heavily trafficked country roads between downtown Palmetto Bay and the beaches. They all said the same thing: "You *know* Bob can do it!"

She shrugged and I picked up the cups, weaving my way between her and my desk to the larger living room. We settled on the couch and chair with our coffee and I turned on the stereo for some background music but got the beginning of Red Flannery's "Talk-to-Me-America Show," a nationwide radio talk show heavily flavored by Red's opinions, whether the conversation was on UFOs, auto repairs, or politics. I turned it off. I suppose I was fidgeting.

I wasn't sure if it was because of the lamplight that now washed her face instead of the sun, but she looked bone-tired and weary. "Mac," she said carefully, "I haven't even told you the whole story yet. The therapist has put Candy through some pretty intense sessions lately, and she's started remembering things. Terrible things."

Katherine stopped as though she'd been unplugged and closed her eyes for a few seconds. When she opened them again they were cloudy and distant, and she looked past me to God knows what. I sipped my coffee and took advantage of the pause to look at her, her lips parted, elbows on her knees. She was naturally dark but didn't look like she spent much time in the sun. There was a yellow tint to her smooth cheeks, not sallow but not right, either. That and her lean face made her look like one of those sad, beautiful Oakie women you see in Depression-era photographs. Her shoulders were full and round under the cream-colored blouse, and there was a proud grace in her posture. I could easily imagine her being Sheevers's friend.

Her teeth were large and white and, of the two in front, one leaned slightly against the other. I watched her face and she was so far away in thought that, as the cacophony of night frogs began their droning prayer for rain, I felt like a voyeur. She finally spoke.

"The day before we left for Las Vegas, three people were killed at Limestone Creek. Do you remember that?"

I nodded. "Yeah."

"There were four people at the creek," she said.

"I know," I said. "The drug pusher on the bike."

"No," she said. "Not him. Candace was there. She saw the whole thing."

"Oh, Jesus."

"Try to imagine," she said, still looking through me. "Fourteen years old, two days after an abortion, and she sees her two best friends murdered. She pushed it so far down that she honestly didn't remember it happened. It's been tearing her apart all these years and, maybe now, she can be healed."

"I hope so." I really did. Katherine sipped her coffee and tried to smile at me. The evening had lasted about fifty years so far.

"I guess I let her down when I caved in to Bob Birk." She turned hard. I've never seen a face that gave away more than hers. "No, I don't guess, Mac; I know I did. Candy had counted on me to save her, and I didn't.

"She lost faith." These last words fell from her lips as she looked down into the coffee cup. I had to cock my head to hear her over the chanting frogs. "We lived about a mile from the creek, and Candy and Carol and Tommy had planted a bunch of marijuana down there. I didn't know; in fact, I just found out about it." She lifted her head and looked at me, but I stayed quiet. "It must have been about ready to harvest. Since we lived so close, Candy was the caretaker, and from what she told Dr. Kuyatt, they had planned to sell it to somebody and go on a shopping spree at the mall. Can you believe it?

"They were just kids. Tommy was fifteen and so was Carol, I think. They were going to buy clothes, Mac." Her hands began to shake, but she settled down and her eyes cleared. "They got together after the . . . after Candy's abortion, and decided to sell the crop and run away together. They didn't want anything more to do with any of us, and I don't blame them." Katherine covered her face with her hands.

As her strength crumbled, her voice took on a pleading tone and I knew she needed support. She was begging for understanding and I just sat there, mute and helpless. She pulled her hands from her face and hugged herself until I finally dug deep and scraped together enough personality to cross over to the sofa. I sat down beside her clumsily, pulled her head to my chest, and leaned back. A deep, sobbing, lonesome cry came from her, sounding like something years in the making. Her hands, bunched together at her breasts, made a hard knot against my ribs.

As she cried, a thorn of irritation made it impossible for me to think rationally about Katherine Furay and her anguish. After a few minutes she stiffened and her tears stopped. She coughed and wiped her eyes on my shirt, then put her palms against my chest and pushed herself upright. Her eyes were puffy and apologetic. "This isn't me," she said. "I don't cry."

"Boy, I do," I said. "I cry at card tricks."

[17]

"I haven't been away from Candy in years, Mac, and I don't think I've ever known this kind of pain," she said. "She's been hurting for so long, and I want it to be over." Her eyes stayed wet, and I could hear her teeth grinding together. "It's never going to be over."

"Why don't we call it a night?" I said, hoping I sounded kind. "I'm sure someone's waiting and worrying about you too."

"Nobody here even knows me anymore," she said. I couldn't believe that. "I have a room at the La Quinta, but I'm in no hurry to get back. I would like to call home, though." She put her hands together.

"Why don't you just call from here?" I said, suddenly wanting her to linger. I leaned away from her and pulled a clean T-shirt from the laundry basket that usually serves as my combination closet and chest of drawers. I'm very informal at home.

"Wipe your face," I said, and she did.

"You don't mind?" she said.

"No." I lifted my rotary phone from the end table and placed it in her lap. A light rain swept up the sidewalk and tapped on the windows. "But I have to ask you something first. You said they were trying to sell dope to Renaldo Tippit and not the other way around?"

"Mac, please listen closely. That's why I'm here." She put a hand on mine. "According to Candy, Renaldo Tippit wasn't even there. They were selling the grass to the other guy, Pete Mullins. Candy said Tommy knew him and they took him out there to show him the plants. That's how dumb they were.

"Anyhow, Candy was already there. She walked to the creek from the house, and the plan was for her to hide up the path, and if the guy did anything funny, she was supposed to shoot into the air with my four-ten." Katherine shook her head in disbelief, and I tried to imagine a frightened fourteen-year-old girl hiding in the dark with a small, loaded shotgun. "I was in town, trying to get everything together for the trip. I was so ashamed, I didn't even tell Patty what I was doing. My cousin lived in Las Vegas, and as far as I knew, she was the only relative I had left. So I decided to go there."

A sudden gust of wind rattled the tin on my roof and I heard someone's trash can tumbling down the street. The rain began to fall harder, and its roar on my roof ended the song of the frogs.

"Have you ever been to the creek?" she asked, and I tried to remember. It was popular with the canoe and inner-tube crowd, but spring water's too cold for me and I avoid it. I had driven over it a few times, though, and I told her that. "Well, you know the big fence that

[18]

runs along the other side? It's covered with huge pieces of tin and it's really ugly."

"Yeah," I said. "I've seen it. That's all Omni property over there, isn't it?" Omni, Inc., was a consortium of Panhandle business and community leaders, and the tract of twenty thousand or so acres was protected from taxes by the Greenbelt Laws. Private, armed guards protected it from everything else. There were private hunt clubs and two shallow, landscaped lakes surrounded by luxury retreats, including tennis courts and driving ranges, or so I'd heard. It was probably an innocent mistake, but I wasn't on any of the guest lists.

There was also, according to rumor, a large and sumptuous complex called the Limestone Creek Men's Club, where the powers-that-be dodged the Florida Sunshine Laws once a month to play poker and divide up the Panhandle among themselves. Family fortunes and political careers had supposedly been won and lost there.

"I think it's all Omni's," she said. I draped an arm over the back of the sofa and my hand touched her hair. "Anyhow, Candy was hiding beside one of the pieces of tin on the fence while Tommy and Carol were talking to the Mullins man, and she said Tommy stopped talking and ran over to the fence. Candy said he yelled, 'What the hell are you doing?'—or something like that—then she heard someone shooting really fast and Tommy fell over on his back. Carol ran over to Tommy and started crying, and a bright light came on. She said there was a bunch of yelling in Spanish, and Pete Mullins started to run away and they shot him, too."

The hand that covered mine was squeezing my fingers together very hard, and I held my breath, trying not to anticipate the next part of the story, but my mind was full of Colombian dope squads and mountains of cocaine. When I looked at Katherine I could literally see her heartbeat drumming against the thin fabric of her blouse. "Someone pulled part of the fence away and Candy saw about a dozen soldiers in camouflage army uniforms come through the hole," Katherine said.

"Wait a minute," I said. "Is she positive they were speaking Spanish?"

"My mother was Spanish," she said. "I taught Candy to speak it when she was little."

"Oh," I said. "Sorry to interrupt."

"That's okay." Her hand loosened its grip and my fingers tingled. "But, Mac, all this came out in therapy and it was very controlled.

"Let me finish," she said. The wind had stopped, and rain fell gently. "She said a soldier with a flashlight ran up and down the path

[19]

and looked everywhere for someone else. He came just a few feet from Candy, and she told Dr. Kuyatt she pointed the gun at him." Katherine shivered.

"She heard somebody call him back and tell him the major was coming, and they got very quiet. Then a tall, blond man in a uniform walked up and said in English, 'What have you done, you stupid bastards.' He talked into a radio—Candy said it looked like a shiny black box with a telephone on top. She couldn't hear any of what he said, or else she still can't remember it, but she said when he put the phone back he talked to the other soldiers in Spanish and told them to turn off the lights.

"Oh, Mac." She leaned back, and I stroked her hair. Tears escaped her dark lashes and left silver trails, and she didn't try to stop them. "Candy said they turned off the lights but the moon was so bright they didn't really need them. Carol was on her knees beside Tommy, and the blond soldier walked over to her and just pulled out his pistol and shot her in the head."

The air around us turned cold, and my hand stopped moving. I tried to swallow but couldn't. When Katherine finally continued, her voice was small and soft. "Dr. Kuyatt told me to go to Senator Teall in Las Vegas and tell him what happened, but I'm scared. You've always been in my mind as the one person I could turn to, because of all the things Patty told me, so I came here first.

"Help me, Mac," she said.

THREE

I got to my feet and walked to the door. Moisture and the cool night air combined to swell the wooden door against the jamb, and I experienced a mild case of panic when I tugged on the brass knob and nothing happened. I needed air. I yanked again and the door came free, drawing the damp night inside to swirl around me like a cold ocean wave. I leaned against the screen door and took a deep breath.

I've always loved early spring in the Florida Panhandle. It's too early for jasmine and gardenia, but the wind is always spiced with tender dogwood and lingering wisteria, and rain brings out scents of wild onion and new grass. Wild plum blossoms, just turning pink in a halo of shiny green leaves, breathe their fragrance into the bouquet until the air is almost an intoxicant, and is always a balm. Or so I thought.

I gasped for breath like a drowning man, but I could find no peace. I had sunk these last few years into a comfortable Zen state that effectively blocked out anything I didn't want to face—all those things I used to rail about with Sheevers, finger in the air as I accused the world while she applauded. Meddling in the business of other countries, tampering with the environment, or ruining the economy. I had answers to them all and opinions on everything. The murders at Limestone Creek happened during a time of intense change in northwest Florida, and we snorted with disgust at each trainload of tanks and artillery that passed through Palmetto Bay to the ports where they were loaded onto big ships and taken into obscurity, unnoticed by the press.

Stories of secret training bases for Central American rebels were pooh-poohed by the government and, in the papers, given the same respect granted people who wrote in to report flying saucers. It still seemed too farfetched for me, especially considering the amount of land the military owns around here. Why risk doing something like that on private property? Of course, there are favors and back-scratch-ings and political considerations to take into account at any time, and this was a time for chest beating and flag waving. I just couldn't think clearly, and I wished I had stayed a little bit more in practice.

"She can't remember anything else," Katherine said. "Even under hypnosis. There's no recall. When I got home that night she wasn't there, and I was afraid she'd run away. She hadn't talked much to me since the abortion. I sat home and watched the door until she came in about three o'clock in the morning, covered with mud and crying, and I had to strip her down and bathe her before I could put her to bed. All she would say was she'd been out walking."

I looked at Katherine over my shoulder, and she seemed smaller, dwarfed by the high-backed couch. Where Sheevers had been round and voluptuous, the color of light honey with vinegar eyes, Katherine was stately and dark, her eyes almost always in shadows. She didn't move as I stared.

"Why don't you go ahead and call her, Katherine." I stayed formal but couldn't stop myself from a commitment. "We'll figure out where to start later."

It wasn't direct or forceful, but she looked relieved and her smile was like a kiss. She nodded, and as she dialed, I wandered into the kitchen with the coffee cups, trying to contain a strange and complex set of emotions. She cleared her throat as I drifted toward the hall. I pulled at my collar and ran a hand across my hair.

"Hello?" Her voice took on a lilt. "James? It's me. . . . Yes, I've missed you, too." I stopped, and my heart shot blood through me like a lawn sprinkler. My fingers touched the wall.

"What?" She laughed. "Yes, it's going to be okay." A pause. "I love you, too. Let me talk to Candy."

I stepped into the bathroom and closed the door, propped my hands on the sink, and avoided the mirror. I felt Sheevers beside me where I knew she would always be, and I let her arms embrace me, felt her cheek on my back. "I'm sorry," I whispered to her, and carefully dropped to my knees, my fingers caressing the cold tiles where she died for me. I swore to her then that I would find the ones who took her precious life, and I felt a resolve like the first kindling of an angry fire somewhere deep inside.

I became aware of a pain in my knees and a muscle jumped in my thigh. My toes were cramped inside my shoes and I felt dizzy, reaching out to grasp the sink again, but this time for support. I looked at my watch and it was one-twenty. Sounds of light rain came from the small, dark window above my tub. I stood slowly, wincing as my knees and ankles popped, then opened the bathroom door and stepped quietly back into the hall. The front door still stood open, and at first I thought she'd gone, but when I walked into the living room I saw her lying on the sofa. She had one arm tucked under her head, her cheek pushed against it, her lips pursed. The other arm hung over the side, fingers still touching the phone. One leg stretched the length of the cushions and her skirt was bunched around her thighs. Those eyes were smooth and at peace in her sleep, and the effect was startling. She looked like a child. I went into my bedroom and came back with a light quilt, covered her, removed her shoes, and closed the front door without seeing her move.

I was into my second cup of coffee, and the early-morning sun was turning my wet lawn into a field of diamonds when I heard her call out from the sofa.

"In here," I said. "Want some coffee?"

"In a minute." Her voice was thick, and she sounded disoriented. Her feet slapped heavily in the hall and I heard the bathroom door close. I poured a steaming cupful of coffee and slid it across the table. I debated whether to toss the morning paper into a drawer, but there was no need to start this job off wearing kid gloves, so I left it on the table. The headline was bold: "BIRK NEXT GOVERNOR?"

Actually, the question mark at the end was a surprising bit of temerity, almost an editorial in itself in a town where Birk held such a large percentage of the advertising.

"Time-zit?" she mumbled as her hand cupped my head. She pushed off and made it to the chair.

"Seven-fifteen," I said, glancing at my watch.

"God." She scooped up the cup, and her face almost disappeared behind a cloud of steam when she breathed.

We sat in silence as we drank. I saw her stop in midsip and turn her head to the side, her eyes locking in on the front page. "What's that?" she said, her voice flat and dry.

"That's nails for breakfast," I said. "If you want to win this one, you're going to have to learn to eat them."

"I'll do anything if it'll destroy this monster." Katherine took one hand from her cup and jabbed at Birk's photograph.

"Anything?" I said, trying to match her tone. "How about facing reality for starters. Can you do that?"

"Pardon me?" I had caught her by surprise.

[23]

"Reality," I said. "I've been sitting here for over an hour trying to fit the pieces together, but there's one that doesn't go, no matter which way I turn it."

I put my cup down and slid it aside. "What was a fourteen-year-old girl doing at the Sunset Hotel with Bob Birk?"

Her lips got thin. "What exactly are you implying?"

"Tommy Lovett paid girls your daughter's age to turn tricks for the big shots at the Sunset."

"You bastard!" She took a swing at me, and I slapped her hand away.

"I'm an expert on Tommy Lovett and his business," I said. "That's what I was working on when they came in here and killed Sheevers. Right in there." I pointed.

"That's not relevant here." Ice grew in the corners of her eyes. "And, from now on, you can keep your sleazy opinions to yourself."

"It's more than an opinion," I said. "It's fact. You told me Candy and her friends were growing dope to sell for pocket money. I can't remember anymore how hungry a fourteen-year-old can get. I do know you were a single mother living in a little trailer and working your ass off for peanuts. I'm saying you might need to give yourself room for that possibility. We can't afford to make any mistakes."

"I think I may have already made my mistake," she said through her teeth. "There really might not be anything left in you. I think I came to the wrong man." She'd spilled coffee; and I wiped it up with a cloth.

"No, you came to the right man," I said. "I'm the only man in the whole world who hates these people more than you. And I'm the only man in this part of the world that has a chance in hell of making them pay for what they've done. But we're going to start this relationship off with an understanding. We both want revenge, but these people are very dangerous and if we lie to each other we're going to die. They'll just have a good laugh and keep on doing what they do."

"I don't lie," she said.

"Everybody lies." I poured us both another cup of coffee, but she didn't touch hers. "We even lie to ourselves. But you and I are going to tell each other the truth. Your daughter's life may depend on it. All I want you to do is think about this from all angles. I don't give a shit about how it happened, and I don't think you should, either. I just don't want things to start falling down around us when this gets hot. Believe me, Katherine, it's going to get hot."

The incongruity of a bright morning sun and happily chirping birds just outside the window wasn't lost on either of us as we sat entrenched at opposite ends of the tiny table. The legendary me was shrinking to human proportions, and it was hard on both of us. There, for just a little while, it felt good to be a champion. I've always wanted to be one. Katherine stood, pushed the chair back, and walked quietly from the room, I heard her shuffling into her shoes and I thought she was leaving, but she walked back to the table and sat down. She had a photograph in her fingers, and she placed it over Birk's front-page profile. There, with the desert in the background, was a beautiful young woman with dark hair, tinted red by the sun. Her olive complexion highlighted the deep-green eyes and full mouth, and, except for the chipmunk cheeks, she looked a lot like her mother.

"Candace," I said, looking into that young face that had seen so much grief. Katherine lifted her cup and sipped. I took a step backward with my mind and fell into a powerful vortex.

In the peculiar fashion of my brain, I stood before a revolving collage of characters and events, flashes of various locations, and snippets of conversation that slowly and painstakingly arranged themselves into a correct chronology as I rejected this and expanded that.

Ever since I was a child, I've had the ability to find missing articles, not by clairvoyance but because I had the talent of arranging facts and looking into that darkness for gaps others couldn't see. To me they were like missing teeth in an otherwise beautiful smile. By the time I was in high school, kids paid me real money to find things they'd lost and, because of my ability to see these things, the army guessed I would make a great point man. When I'd survived that, they made me a tunnel rat.

What I saw at the breakfast table was a board game for lemmings. It was one of those mazes that offered a dozen ways to begin, but they all merged to a single downhill slide into a black hole. I twisted and turned, pulled things from one place and stuck them in another, and still the ending was the same.

I tried adding new elements as you would add a pink queen to a chess game, an unpredictable player that could work for either side. The board was getting cluttered, and it occurred to me that I hadn't reached this deep in a long time. It might not work anymore. Or it was just possible the process was working fine but I didn't want to believe the conclusions. My mind said I couldn't win.

"Mac!" Katherine's nervous shout revived me and I became aware of her anxious eyes. They were locked on mine.

"What?" I said.

[25]

"What do you mean, 'what?' " she said, funny without trying to be funny.

"Well, then, how about 'huh?' " She didn't seem to be mad at me anymore, and I was glad. I suppose part of the reason I jumped at her so hard over coffee was that I got my feelings hurt the night before, and, after my great speech about honesty and truth, I decided not to tell her.

"I've been trying to talk to you for a couple of minutes," she said. "And you were gone. It scared me."

"I was thinking," I said.

"That wasn't thinking," Katherine corrected me, and her eyes were all I could see. "You were in a trance. Mac, you're a little bit frightening."

"You just raised me from Hell, Katherine Furay," I said. "What did you expect?" I pushed back from the table. "I want to tell you something. Now that I'm here, I plan to keep going until I get these people, whether you back out or not. And that's exactly what I want you to do if you're not prepared to take this to the end. People are going to get hurt before it's over, and I can't promise it won't be you, or Candace.

"I will promise you I won't go back to Hell without company," I finished. I watched her fragile personality bounce again. She rebounded with a smile and a shrug in an attempt to lighten things up.

"I'd feel a lot better about this if you didn't keep talking about doom," she said.

"That's my favorite ending," I said. "It's the only way it can work for me. I'm in love with a dead woman, remember?"

"Yes," she said. She stood up again and walked to the window. Her cup fogged the panes. "I remember."

FOUR

Katherine drove back to her room to shower and change, but made me promise to meet her for lunch at The Coffee Cup restaurant beside the interstate. We sat at a table by the window and watched cars and trucks race past. She was in flowers, a white sundress with red hibiscus and big green leaves that exposed her brown shoulders and colored her cheeks. Her hair was pulled back and held by a red barrette, and her neck was a mile long.

"Have you thought any more about it?" she asked.

"You're kidding, right?" I said. A trucker laughed across the counter at a waitress, and she placed a kind hand on his shoulder and smiled.

"Stupid thing to say, huh?" Katherine's voice was lighter and had hope poured over it.

"I've already started the ball rolling," I said, feeling better myself. She raised an eyebrow. "I made a few phone calls to a few friends. Katherine, there are some good people in this town, and they feel bad about what happened to Sheevers—to Patty. There are a couple of people I know who happen to be in positions to notice changes quicker than most. I've asked them to let me know if anything starts coming down."

"What do you think is going to happen?" She looked worried, and it clashed with the dress. I reached across the table and put my hand on hers.

"There are a few things I'm sure of." I smiled and patted the hand. "I'm not worried about them, and you shouldn't be, either. After you leave I'm going to start shaking some trees, including the big one Birk lives in. That's not going to make any of them very happy, especially when they see who's doing the shaking." I tried to sound confident and loose, and I think I pulled it off. Katherine seemed relaxed as she sipped her Coke, leaving a thin red ring of lipstick on the straw.

[27]

"The first thing I did was call my lawyer. He's a brilliant guy named Mark Thornton, and he'll be in touch with you pretty soon to get your deposition. I don't know why he hangs around this swamp, but he's damned good." She pulled out a notepad and wrote down his name, then put the pen tip to her lips and rolled it back and forth.

"I've heard of him," she said. "I think Patty mentioned him."

"Good," I said. I tried for about the fifth time to follow it through in my mind. "The way I have it figured, Bob Birk's first move will be to have Patty's murder case reopened and he'll pull some strings to have me hauled in as the main suspect. That would pretty much take care of me for the duration, but Mark's going to make a trip to Judge Pollock first and tell him I have some hard facts on Birk involving sex with a minor and he believes Birk will do this as retaliation.

"Pollock hates Bob Birk and he's scared he'll make governor, but he's never been able to screw him, so this might give him the chance. It's not that the judge is a great guy. They're more like leaders of rival gangs."

"That doesn't sound like a sure thing to me, Mac," Katherine said. Her fingers wormed their way between mine and she locked us together. Her hand felt a little like a cold oyster, and, even in the bright light of the restaurant, there seemed to be a shadow over her. "Now that I've done it, I'm afraid."

"This is one of those things you can't turn your back on, Katherine," I said. "It took a lot of courage for you to come this far."

"That wasn't courage," she said. "It was just more fear. Aren't you afraid of what will happen?"

"No." Lie number two. "I already have a pretty good idea of what I'm going to do." Number three. I was on a roll.

"And what is that?" she said.

"I told you I've already started the process. You never find something out by chasing it around and trying to catch up to it. It has a head start and it'll outrun you every time." I felt myself warming to the subject, and it was a good sensation. "You have to set a trap for it and then encourage it to fall in. That's what I've done by calling a couple of people, Katherine. I have no idea if I'll hear from any of them, but simply having them there changes things. The subtle changes in them may encourage others to come to me, to the trap.

"This time, though, it'll be more like an earthquake. Part of what I did with the phone calls this morning was to set a line of human seismographs along a fault line. The next thing I'll try to do is create a little earthquake, then trace the tremors back to the epicenter." I looked at her and saw genuine interest. "It's actually a pretty good analogy. You see, we're starting off with a serious deficit of information. I want to know exactly whose ground shakes the hardest, then I can find out why. That's the reason the early part of this thing has to be a risk. It has to be, because it's a smoke screen, pure and simple."

I looked around casually to see if anyone was listening. There were a few people scattered through the restaurant, mostly travelers in wrinkled clothing and matted hair. The waitresses were occupied, and it wasn't so busy that our loitering was a bother. Besides, there was still food on our table and a potential tip to be had later. With the skimpy salary these women made, a tip of any size had to be taken into consideration.

"I want everyone to think I'm building a case against Bob Birk for rape and contributing to the delinquency, because I don't want anyone to know we have an eyewitness to murder. You see, Birk has his hands in everything and this is all connected somehow. I don't see it yet, but I have to get to them first. I'll only have one chance.

"Katherine, you have to put the personal part of yourself aside now and listen. I know how you feel about Birk, but he's not even a gnat compared to the company we're going to keep if we get far enough to find out who killed Candy's friends." An eighteen-wheeler growled through its gears as it climbed the on-ramp.

There was an honest-to-goodness smile on Katherine's face. It swept across her cheeks like a brush fire, and her eyes sparkled as it turned into a grin. I felt my ears get hot and knew they were turning red. "I have just witnessed the most amazing thing," she said, her voice like music. "I wish you could see it for yourself, Mac—the part that makes you so good at what you do. I've just seen a spark of what Patty used to spend hours talking about."

"A cheap parlor trick," I mumbled. I thought of how Sheevers and I would spend days driving bumpy orange clay roads the color of Irish hair, noticing everything and discussing what kind of old farmhouse we'd want, how many animals we'd have. I remembered the time we stopped the car and made love in the daylight like idiots, fully expecting someone to drive by and get offended. But no cars came and I swore to her that I'd never love another woman. Then, for some reason, that picture was obscured by the image of a frightened young girl with a gun.

"I don't know how yet," I said to Katherine Furay, "but I'm going to beat them. I'm going to make them pay for what they did."

"Thanks for making me believe it, Mac," she said.

[29]

We pushed food around on our plates a little longer and wrapped up our noncontract, agreeing that she would go back to Las Vegas and make plans to disappear with Candace when the time came. She wanted to bring her daughter back to hide somewhere close by and I thought it was a lousy idea, if for no other reason than the chance of exposing Candace to the old crowd, the old memories. I was also afraid they'd be discovered by someone in Birk's network. I thought if everything went well I could possibly keep the different elements from knowing how much I had on them until it was too late to stop me, but all I had on my side was surprise. I wasn't sure if that would even be enough for the ante.

I told Katherine my idea of going to see an old friend of mine, although, in the last few years, our friendship had turned more and more into an adversarial relationship. He was an extremely caustic man three decades older than I who had gone from beatnik to magazine publisher in a little over thirty years without changing values once. He had the fractious nature of someone who hated everyone, including me. But, other than that, he was a reasonable man.

Mel Shiver had once been a fairly important liberal, and he watched the world change around him, affecting it about as much as a tree stump affects floodwaters. He'd always been too much a loner to join a group and form a dam, and, eventually, the groups began rejecting him as well. Still, he published a very good literary quarterly called *Walker's Companion* with a staff of one, a kind woman who doubled as his wife. He lived outside Red Oak, a tiny town thirty miles northeast of Palmetto Bay, and he had his own network of information. His "Baker Street Irregulars" consisted of intellectual flotsam that bobbed carelessly in the wake of the flood.

I always thought he had too little character to be a curmudgeon, so he had to settle for being an ordinary asshole, and I told him so on occasion. Another acquaintance from the courthouse days, he and I had been fighting for years over almost everything—unofficial sparring partners for life. Lately, he'd been mad at me because he wanted me to contribute to his Middle East peace fund and I told him that, as far as I was concerned, the Middle East was just the Hatfields and the McCoys on steroids and I thought they were silly. Sometimes I believed what I said, and sometimes I just made things up to make him mad.

Mel had filed so many freedom-of-information suits over the years that his paperwork was almost invisible to the government, or at least that's what I hoped. Beneath his well-maintained front, he was as completely decent and honorable as anyone I'd ever known, and I planned to dump this whole thing on him, right down to the last detail. Each hour I had to think brought me closer to an inevitable conclusion. I didn't stand a Gregorian's chance in Hell alone, and there were precious few people on the planet I could trust. Mel Shiver was on the top of my short list.

I followed Katherine to the airport and waited as she turned in her rental car, then stood with her in the small terminal and argued until her flight arrived. She wanted to stay an extra day and go to Mel's with me, and I was afraid someone would see us together and gain a step on us. I finally convinced her my way was better, and she took her place in line at the baggage counter. We said our good-byes and I hurried away, suddenly restless and in a hurry to get started.

Alone, my bravado abandoned me and I went to the lounge instead of the car. I ordered a drink and took it to a window table where I could see her plane. My thoughts turned against me and the plan began to look like a straw house. I tried to think positively, but my mind turned to the little girl in the dark, a witness to murder so cold it made my stomach muscles draw up. A fourteen-year-old girl hiding in the dark with a gun, suddenly outnumbered and at war in her own backyard.

Then the inevitable image crept in as I knew it would. When my thoughts turned to Katherine with the mysterious eyes I saw Patty Sheevers instead, her blouse ripped open and that electric body doughy, white, and limp, pocked with grotesque open holes. Her eyes protruding and full of terror, even in death. I heard the ice rattling in my glass and put down the drink.

If there were any flaws in my hasty plans, if I got reckless and cocky, someone would die. With any luck it would be me, but I don't have that kind of luck. I'm more like Typhoid Mary and the people around me are the ones at risk. I knew Bob Birk kept a few people in the wings who took care of unpleasant things like me, and I knew that somewhere, early on, I would make him mad enough to use them. I hadn't yet come up with a plan to deal with that, and it was just a little problem when you held it up to the big picture.

The plane finally rolled out onto the runway, roared a bit, and rose gracefully into a cloudless sky. I gulped the last of my drink and walked quickly from the cool, dark building into the sun. I retrieved my clump of keys from a pocketful of change and crossed to a full parking lot, eyeing every stranger's face with suspicion. Katherine had pulled me from under a nice, comfortable rock, and I wanted to shrink

[31]

from the light. When I swung open my car door I heard someone inside the car say, "I thought you'd never get here."

I yelled something that sounded like "Yar!" and threw my keys straight into the air before Katherine could say, "Uh-oh."

I clutched my chest and sat down hard on the vinyl seat, glaring at her for at least a minute before the keys fell back with a clatter on my hood. She covered her mouth with her hands, but I could tell by her eyes what was going on back there. The beautiful jerk was laughing at me. I reached out and grabbed my keys.

"Jesus Christ! Has anyone ever told you that it's hard as hell to get rid of you?"

I was really humiliated. A full day of acting like Manly Man, and just when I thought I could relax, my true self burst forth like pastel fireworks. An idle thought crossed my mind that it might take surgery to get my balls back down into their normal position.

She tried to talk but could say only, "Oh . . . oh." Then she snorted and buried her face in my sleeve. Thank God I wasn't wearing my heart there, or it would have beaten her to death.

Katherine finally got it out of her system and flowed backward until she was wedged into the corner made by the seat and the door. Somewhere above, an airplane with one empty seat banked on a cushion of warm Gulf air and turned north toward Atlanta.

"I'm sorry," she said, not sounding at all as if she meant it. She sniffed and looked out the windshield as she ran a fingertip under one eye, then the other. "I just kept thinking that you'd need me there, you know, to explain everything."

"Katherine," I said. "Are you trying to avoid going home?"

"No," she said, still looking away. "Well, yes. Maybe."

"Good," I said. "For a minute there I was afraid you were going to be indecisive."

"It's hard, Mac." She turned to me. "It's like living in a mine field right now. I'm a good mother, but Candy's a grown woman, too, and sometimes the house is just too small. I want to run away, do you know what I mean?"

"I'd live on the moon if I could find a way to get there," I said. "What about James?"

"James?" Katherine looked at me, puzzled, then smiled. "Oh, I forgot," she said. "I talked to him on the phone last night at your house." She folded her hands in her lap, her lips forming words for a few seconds before she actually spoke. "James has been very good to me, Mac, and Candy too.

"I've been working in a casino for years, and sometimes it gets wild. I started as a waitress in the lounge, worked up to the blackjack tables, and now I'm in management. But you still have to deal with the crazies at any level. The funny thing is, the whole operation is backward. The casino is on the up-and-up and the executives are conservative and straight, but the preachers and the schoolteachers come there and go nuts at the tables. They keep doing 'white paper' reports on the news about organized crime, but I'm just thankful it's organized." She seemed to have taken a trip there while she talked, and she drifted back to me.

"James has given both of us stability and a home. Lately, that hasn't been easy." She sounded uncomfortable, and I was close to punching a hole in my palm with the car key. She brushed a hand across her forehead.

"Well, listen," she said. "There's another flight at nine tonight. I know you're calling the shots on this, but I'm so used to making my own decisions. I guess this was a bad one."

"No, not really," I said. "It'll make it a lot easier on me to have you do the talking. Did I tell you Mel doesn't like me?" She nodded. "If we can get him interested he may be able to plug in to a pretty high level of contacts. Without him, I don't think we can pull it off.

"I'll have you back in time to catch that plane," I said.

FIVE

Katherine used the ride to get reacquainted with the lush jungle that is northwest Florida. Low black ponds guarded by prehistoric cypress were all that separated miles of slash pines, all in neat rows that chopped the sun into a dizzying strobe of light. Huge spider webs stretched between trees and reflected its brilliant colors. Open, rolling pastures dotted with mossy oaks and thick, healthy cattle separated the low clapboard homes with rusted tin roofs, their yards filled with farm machinery and old cars, mostly hidden behind tall green dog fennel and stacks of used tires. She bristled at the billboards that proclaimed Bob Birk as a fighter for the "Little Guy." Now that he had formally declared his candidacy for the gubernatorial race, his campaign had gone into overdrive.

Birk had risen fast during the eighties and didn't even stumble as he crossed into the next decade. A friend of presidents and a leader of men, the billboards said. He made the noises of a populist, positioning himself always as the patriot and as the friend of "good people" all over Florida. The man who struggled against "big government" and the tax-and-spend liberals in Washington. The old stories of his questionable fortunes were weeded out by clever public relations agencies, and by time. He was becoming a local hero—the champion of every blood drive, the guy with a temperature of 102, who gets out of bed at three in the morning to deliver a check for just enough money to push the total over the top and save the telethon. The man I was going to challenge to a duel.

They say that in the Panhandle you can stand in mud up to your neck and dust will blow in your face, and when we turned off the pitted highway to Mel's house the truth in the axiom was evident. Even after a night of rain the clay was powdery and hung thick and red in the still air. An approaching car created a dust storm.

I pulled through the gate to Mel's property and blew the horn,

[34]

pointing as his two huge German shepherds crawled from under the porch and ran barking across the yard. The house was a low wood frame structure that had spread haphazardly from its original three rooms to become a testament to Mel's whimsy. The dogs were tall enough to look straight into the windows of the car, and I rolled mine down a little and said, "Hey, Sack-o!" The dog's quizzical, intelligent eyes shifted and his tail began to sway.

"Who's this?" Katherine had shrunk from the window.

"Van Zeti, of course," I said, and she laughed.

"Of course," she said. "Hello, Van." His bark had dropped to the woof level by the time we rolled to a stop under a large pecan tree, its new leaves thick and shiny green. The house had probably once been white, but now was pretty much the same color as the clay road. As I climbed out and scratched Sack-o under the collar, a menacing voice from the shadows of the screened porch growled. "What do you want?"

"It's me, Mel," I said. "McDonald Clay."

"I know," his familiar voice crackled. "That's why I want to know what you want."

"Damn," I said as Van Zeti leaped on me and I rubbed his side. I swam through the dogs to Katherine's door and helped her out. The dogs sniffed her, and she touched them cautiously.

"I need your help, Mel," I said.

"Don't give me that crap, Clay." I knew he could be volatile, and I'd given him reasons to be over the years. He had loved Sheevers, and, before she died, we would sit for hours on his porch watching cardinals wink by in flashes of red while his cats looked up and tried to compute the wind speed and the birds' forward velocity. Gardenias and camellias protected the sides of his house, and giant azaleas, now brilliant in pink and magenta, stood sentinel along the rangy fence and were a cool home to a couple of large black snakes. In the deep part of summer, when a cloud couldn't be bought with gold, Mel kept us in gallons of iced tea in giant, sweating glasses.

He had yelled at me when Sheevers and I drove up to tell him about the state's attorney's offer to hire me to bust Tommy Lovett. He called me a fool. We were so swelled with pride in our newfound respectability that we didn't take him seriously. Mel slapped each word out of the way in a staccato outburst. "You're going to regret doing this, you fuzzy-headed son of a bitch! I never took you for a fool!"

Now, like parents whose only child died in a senseless accident, we were bonded forever in an angry union. Mel Shiver had never

[35]

mentioned Sheevers to me again after her death, but our sparring had taken on a bitter edge that his wife, Torrea Levi-Shiver, would not tolerate.

"Get out of the way, old man!" I could hear her scolding Mel from the porch as Katherine listened in silence. The screen door screeched open and slammed against the wall, and Torrea came through the opening like a cannonball. Three cats on the steps ran into each other trying to get out of her way. Her arms were open and her face was an advertiser's dream. In her middle sixties, Torrea had snow-white hair and red cheeks like little apples, bifocal glasses propped on a pixie nose, and a mind and personality like Molly Yard. I was in awe of her, and she not only knew it, she loved it.

"McDonald!" She smiled at me and winked at Katherine. She wrapped her arms around my waist and crushed me. "I have missed you!" Each word she spoke was measured and important.

"And who are you?" She turned to Katherine, leaving me wheezing and overjoyed by her presence. She would know everything about Katherine by the time they came in from the yard, so I turned my attention to her husband, still lurking in the shadows.

"Mel?" I knew that there would be no banter, that something was wrong. I got no answer, and when I stepped up into the porch, he wasn't there. I walked through the open door and into his house, each familiar room a treacherous mountain range of books and magazines, teetering high above the modest furnishings. A bank of televisions flashed without sound in the corner beside his giant, computer-filled desk, and, from the radio, Red Flannery was lecturing a caller on the virtues and dangers of investing in the stock market. Mel sat at the dining-room table with his back to me.

"Listening to Flannery? Mel, I'm a bit surprised." I tried to float it in like a paper airplane.

"Red's an old friend of mine," Mel said with an angry rhythm. "I've known him a hell of a lot longer than I've known you."

That really did surprise me, as did Mel's lingering animosity. That was usually slow to develop, even in our most spirited exchanges. I walked around a stack of plastic milk crates filled with computer paper and saw a cane propped against the yellow Formica table, its gnarled brown wood reflected in the table's chrome trim. Mel was still silent, but the enormous cast that had swallowed his left leg spoke volumes. Even close to seventy years old, he was a physical man and very proud. He explained the virtual armory of weapons in his house to me once by saying only that he was a "rural liberal."

[36]

"What's that?" I'd said. I knew he loved to hunt on his one-hundred-acre spread.

"A rural liberal is a liberal with a gun," he'd said.

I walked slowly into the dining room and stood beside the table. "Sorry, Mel."

"Sorry?" He didn't turn around. "What the hell are you sorry for?"

"Melvin!" The sharp bark of his name from behind me startled both of us, and Torrea walked in, arm in arm with a smiling Katherine. She seated the younger woman at the opposite end of the table from Mel and waved me over. "McDonald, please have a seat. I'm the host until Melvin's manners heal.

"This is Katherine Furay. She was a friend of Patricia." Her soft words to her husband brought his head around to Katherine, and I watched his face come to life. He looked pale and weak, and I realized then that his age was as much a factor as the cast on his leg. I held my tongue as I sat down.

"Hello, Katherine," he said, his voice full and rich. "Please forgive me. I'm suffering from the very first broken bone I've ever had, and it seems to have affected my civility. I'm so used to dealing with this bonehead that I didn't notice he was bringing real company." He was still calling me names, but his approach to her was gentle and I hoped the tension had passed.

She smiled at him, and I could see him loosen up. I already knew the healing power of that smile and began to believe we might convince Mel after all. Torrea had never been one to waste time with small talk, and she spun us directly into our business.

"Melvin," she said to her husband, "they have something very important to tell us. I think you should listen closely." Torrea possessed a powerful calm, and when she spoke there was an aura about her that compelled others to pay attention.

"Katherine needs our help, and I believe that all we have here may finally be put to use." Mel raised an eyebrow and leaned toward his wife. "She's only told me a little, Melvin, and it scares me." I think it was hearing her, the one person in my universe that I thought of as a solid rock, talk of being afraid that made me really grasp the scope of our undertaking. I thought I knew what we were up against, but I'd been so busy concentrating on boring my little holes into the case that I never stopped to think of the true size of my opponent. I lost a lot of inertia there at the table.

Torrea touched Katherine's hand. "Would you like some tea?" she asked, and I told her I'd get it. I almost fell out of the chair in my hurry for something cold to drink, my mouth suddenly so dry it was as if it had been swabbed with cotton. I stumbled into the kitchen to the old, round refrigerator, and as I wrapped my hands around a gallon jar filled with chilled, reddish-brown tea, the color of a clear, deep river, I heard Torrea say to Katherine, "It's all right, dear, you just start anywhere."

I cracked enough ice from a white plastic bucket of cubes in the freezer to fill four glasses, found a tray, and poured the glasses to the brim. When I returned to the table Katherine was explaining the events that led up to the murders, and I quietly spread the glasses around and took my seat. She stopped to drink, and I stared at her. She closed her eyes and one hand went to her throat. I glanced at Mel, and he seemed captivated. She finished the glass of tea before she stopped, and I slid mine to her. When she began telling them about the murders at Limestone Creek, Katherine slipped her hand into mine.

I watched her closely, the emotion so close to the surface, and I realized this wasn't an old story. This was new to her, too, and she was still in shock, still confused.

She told it with no interruptions. Mel, a large man with a thick chest and arms like small trees, sat quietly with his elbows on the table, chin on his thumbs as his index fingers bridged his lips closed. He stared at Katherine, and occasionally his black eyes would flick to me before returning to her. When she finished, Katherine closed her eyes and let her head fall back, shaking her thick hair. I watched her flex like a cat, slowly stretching from her neck to her feet before she opened her eyes and glanced at me. A milky cloud seemed to spread under her olive skin.

"Are you okay?" I said. She nodded. Mel stood carefully and pushed the chair back. He swung the plaster-covered leg before him and grasped his cane angrily, half leaning on it and half choking it as he step-shuffle-stepped to a tall, narrow window. He leaned against the stout frame and stared into the yard. Clouds covered the setting sun and his face went gray. Torrea slipped silently into the kitchen, and I could hear the smooth gurgle of tea over ice. She came back with refills and dealt them around the table.

"That is the most frightening thing I have ever heard." Mel's voice was the sound of age with the bass turned all the way up. "Goddamn them! Goddamn the lot of them!" Red Flannery mumbled from the other room as a tinny telephone voice asked him questions.

"I knew they were training the bastards here, but I couldn't prove it. I couldn't get anybody to talk, and I couldn't find anybody who cared if they were bringing them here." He sounded more bitter than I'd ever imagined possible.

"It may be something else," I said. "You know, Cuban mercenaries or some right-wing religious stuff."

"Don't be stupid!" He spit the words at me and turned too fast, tilting dangerously for a second. "You bring me this, put Miss Furay through it, and then you say something as asinine as that? What the hell do you think you're doing, Mac?"

"Looking at all sides?" I suggested. He glared at me, and for a moment, there were just the two of us in the room. The moment dragged on. He propelled himself back to the table.

"Why did she come to you?" Mel said.

"Why don't you ask Katherine?" I wondered if he'd forgotten we used to like each other.

"This one isn't for you, Mac," he said. "Let her take the doctor's advice and go to the government. Let Congress fight it out."

"I don't believe you're saying this, Mel," I said. "You don't believe I can do it, do you?"

"No." His answer was flat and automatic. It landed on me like a hot coal.

"Then again," I tried to stay level, "you didn't think I could do it five years ago, either."

"You didn't," he said. "All you did . . ." He paused and looked away.

"Go ahead, Mel," I said. "Remind me what happened the last time I started a crusade." He looked back at me and the rage was gone, but the cold words didn't stop.

"I don't need to remind you," he said. "Just make sure this woman is safe before you unfurl your banner."

"Nobody's safe, Mel," I said. "You should know that."

I lifted the tea and drank while my stomach jumped back and forth over all the little organs in its neighborhood. Mel's attitude was like a battering ram to my new confidence and I desperately wanted to hide that from Katherine, but it was her faith that came to the rescue. She rose from the chair and stepped behind me.

"Please stop," she said. "I came to Mac because he was the only one I wanted for this. To be honest, I don't think there's any way we can beat them, but my daughter deserves a chance and I'm going to try."

"Me too, Mel," I said. "And I plan to win, with you or without you."

The gathering darkness hid a rolling fog that erased the world beyond each window, and I felt Katherine's hands on my arm as I stood up, still locked in to Mel's gaze. Torrea appeared beside him and rubbed his stomach.

"Mel fell off the barn two weeks ago," she said as though we had just walked in the door and were saying howdy-do's. "And even though he landed on his leg, I suspect it was his brain that took the beating. Please don't go yet." We all stood now, wooden and stiff, until Mel sat with a thump that made the dishes rattle in the cupboard.

"Give me a week and I should have enough to start you off on the right path," he said. "It'll take longer for anything substantial, but I'll put all my effort into it." It was as close to an apology as I would ever get, and I accepted it.

"Thanks," I said. We all dawdled, clumsy and embarrassed, as night fell. The talk was stilted and forced, but we worked out the skeleton of a plan. A place to start. It was over an hour later when we finally made our way to the porch, and as we stepped into the yard the fog pushed us together. It was so thick in the halo of Mel's porch light that when the dogs led the way to my car, it eddied around them like smoke.

Torrea crushed me again and took Katherine's hands as I offered mine to Mel. His eyes dodged mine as he grasped the hand and squeezed. He coughed and said good-bye to Katherine. Four cats were curled together on my hood, and they stared at me in disbelief as I cranked the car, refusing to budge until I put it in gear and drove off, scrunched over the wheel in that idiotic stance you get into when driving in fog, the one in which your mind tells you that if you get closer to the windshield you can see farther. Speed was out of the question, but I was in no hurry. I told myself Mel's age and broken leg had to be taken into account, but the truth was I expected everyone else to come to life simply because I had and it wasn't going to be that easy. I had fallen a long way in five years, and there was no express elevator back. The night was oppressive and damp, and we crept down the road listening to my car rattle on clay that was ridged like a washboard. A rabbit darted in front of me and ran zigzag across the beams of light before leaping over a black ditch.

I eased the car through the fog and reached the airport with an hour to spare. I found a parking place and turned off the engine. The trip had been made in silence as we both retreated into our thoughts. The more we fleshed out the battle plans at Mel's, the more subdued we became until I felt the start of a depression rolling in, not poetically like Sandburg's fog, but heavy, like a manhole cover. A glance at Katherine told me I wasn't alone in trying to dodge it. She turned to me and moved across the seat until we touched. I slipped my hand along her cheek and cupped her head gently.

"I'm driving away this time," I said. "So you'd better really get on that plane."

She nodded against my palm. "Mac, I tried so hard to grow up when Candy was born. I wanted to be independent and strong, and I have been, but a couple of years ago I got so tired of being lonely." I waited for more, but she didn't continue. A pickup truck drove between us and the terminal, and its lights formed long white cones in the fog. The sound of a small airplane engine being cranked and idled came muffled and dull through the open windows.

"I think I know enough about what we're up against to be scared, but I believe in you," she said. "And I know now why Patty did." I swallowed a lump the size of my fist. "I just hope you don't wind up regretting the day you met me."

"That's funny," I said, and my voice sounded alien, like a cartoon. "I was thinking the same thing about you."

I'm not sure if I kissed her or if it was Katherine that started it, but it was sudden and we were both shaken by it. At first it was clumsy and urgent, with the sharp clicking of teeth against teeth, but we made alterations en route and ended up with a pretty smooth finish. We backed away from each other reluctantly, and confusion seemed to be the order of the day. She brushed my lips with her fingers and smiled. There was a long silence.

"I need to give you my phone numbers," she said, but she didn't move. "I usually work from noon to eight, but I'm there off and on and I'm hard to find. It's a big place and it never slows down. There's an answering machine at home." Her eyes wandered down to my shirt. "Just leave a message and I'll get it." She turned in the seat, and I reeled in my hand but couldn't figure out where to put it, so I gripped the wheel. She wrote the numbers in the dark, ripped the page from the pad, and stuffed it in my pocket. "Don't come in," she said. Her hand reached for mine but only touched me. "I'll just make sure there's room on the plane, and if I can get on board, I'll wave at you from the door." She kissed me and slipped out.

"I'll call you soon," she said. We stared at each other, not sure how far to take it. "Be careful."

"You too," I said, and it seemed like a terribly ordinary farewell. She stood and walked away. "Katherine," I called out, and she turned

[41]

expectantly. I really didn't know what else to say, and after a few seconds she blew me a kiss and walked inside. She came to the door after a few minutes and waved toward the car, then disappeared. I sat and watched until the plane rose into the fog, its flashing lights swallowed up before the noise of the engines faded away.

I drove slowly, and when I got to my neighborhood I missed my own road and had to turn around and double back. The driveway was closer than I thought, and I almost drove past it too. The small porch was dark, and I stumbled on the steps. I fumbled through my keys, got the door open, and stepped into my empty house, a place suddenly cold and unfamiliar. Everything was in its place, the aquarium still bubbled, and the fan in my refrigerator still clattered when it stopped. I left a trail of clothes from the sofa to the bedroom and avoided the bathroom door, falling on my unmade bed in a state of utter exhaustion. I held a hand over my face and could smell Katherine's perfume, so I left it there. The world tilted when I closed my eyes, and I fell into a winter day, filled with sunlight.

Thin gray shadows from the naked trees stretched across Patty Sheevers and, like pencil sketches, gave mere suggestion to her form. She smiled, and sunlight danced in her eyes. She looked through strands of yellow hair and noticed me. Warm, moist air that had been deep inside her poured from Patty's parted lips and turned to ice in the winter chill when she said my name. Her voice was such a familiar melody and I ached for her, but we made no effort to touch. I was disoriented and wasn't sure if I was standing up or lying down, or maybe floating somewhere slightly above. But those vinegar-colored eyes had no problem staying locked on mine.

This wasn't a new dream, so my stomach had already knotted up by the time the first wound broke open on her chest. Soon there were more and she begged me to help, but I stayed where I was, watching in horror as she dislocated her shoulders in an attempt to get free of her bonds, eyes wider and wider until I woke up screaming and the telephone rang. I lifted the receiver and apologized to my neighbor, my sweat soaking the mouthpiece. I agreed with the poor man that I really should move someplace else, someplace remote, but we both knew I was resigned to my home like a dragon to his cave.

SIX

"You're a detective?" the rich girl said, then giggled.

The bad thing is, I always knew something was wrong with the Limestone Creek Murders, that someone was going to catch hell for it. I just never imagined it would be me. I stared up at the girl from where I lay on the lawn, her boyfriend's boot tip touching my ear. She was maybe seventeen, but her face looked tired, like she never slept. The makeup, contemptuously applied, didn't help. There's no way, under the circumstances, that I can say I felt sorry for her and not make it sound sarcastic, but I did. Pretty, rich girls are something like sideshow freaks. Their career choices are limited.

"He's not a real detective," I heard a man's voice come from the patio. "He's McDonald Clay." The boyfriend laughed. The man's voice wasn't new to me; I knew him, too—of course, everyone knew his voice. You didn't watch television or listen to radio in Palmetto Bay without hearing him sell his condos, his luxury lakefront lots, his Gulf-front properties. When you watched the local news you heard his political opinions, saw him patting minority children on their heads. He was Bob Birk, of Bob Birk's everything.

Everyone knew his voice, but it was more than familiar to me. Birk's was the first money I ever took to investigate something he didn't want investigated and come up with the conclusion for which he'd paid. I had thought it would be hard, but it wasn't. It was just me then; Sheevers had been long gone. I sat in my office, drank Drambuie, and played dice baseball for five days until they brought me the results of "my" investigation—"proof" that Birk's friend and associate hadn't filled his car lots with hot cars from Alabama, their numbers altered to match serial numbers.

I memorized the facts over the weekend, and on the following Tuesday I sat in the hot seat in circuit court, recited my litany, then stood in the hallway watching their beaming faces as they slapped me on the shoulder and paid me with a check with Bob Birk's logo. I, in turn, made the house payment, paid the bills, and bought groceries. Over a period of time, I became a man who could be counted on to do what he's told, for a price.

Birk pulled me aside one day and said, "Clay, you're an idiot. You always swim against the current. Always. I mean, Christ, don't you ever think to yourself, *What the fuck am I doing?*" I didn't answer, and it made him mad.

"Well, shit," he said. "It's no skin off my ass, but it seems to me that one day you'd wake up and realize no one gives a shit for you. You're no hero. You're just a dumb geek that let his girlfriend get bumped off, and you didn't even do anything about it. Tell you the truth, it embarrasses me to think of you as an American. I mean, what the hell did you ever do for your country?" He rolled his eyes for my benefit.

I shrugged and asked if he wanted me to gas up the truck while I was in town. He told me to get fucked, then he tossed me the gas credit card. I didn't care what he said to me. The only thing that mattered was the check that paid my bills and allowed me to live in the house where Patty Sheevers still walked, where she and I would sit together through the quiet nights and listen to the wind.

Birk's rich daughter looked down at me without emotion. Even the smile was gone. She would never believe there was a time I laughed at men like her father, the man who seemed destined to be Florida's next governor. "Oh." I saw the recognition in her brown eyes. It was as though she'd just scraped me off the bottom of her shoe and found something disgusting. "I've seen you. You work for Daddy."

"Not anymore he doesn't," Birk said. I felt the wet lawn through my suit coat and turned my head to the sound of his voice, looking past his rich daughter. In doing so, I noticed that, except for the distinct jawline that branded her as his own, she was his direct opposite. Where he was short, she was tall; where he was fat, she was thin; he was dark and swarthy and she was fair and smooth, and I knew then that his wife hated him. I'd never met her, but I immediately respected a woman who could stand up to the great Bob Birk and create this act of genetic defiance. I looked in his eyes.

"Have you ever heard of Candace Furay?" I said.

He blinked. "Who?"

"Her girlfriends called her Candy."

Bob Birk looked at the boyfriend. "Help Mister Clay to his feet."

The boyfriend leaned down and grabbed my wrist, pulling me

upright like he was taking up an anchor, then held my elbow as I caught my balance. It seemed fair, since he was the one who knocked me down. After that one punch I was just glad he hadn't caught me a couple of minutes earlier when I was in Birk's office with my hands in the safe.

"So that's the reason you were sneaking around my house?" Birk said. "Looking for some bitch?"

"I wasn't aware I was sneaking," I said.

"Shut up," Birk said. "You caused all this trouble just to ask me something you could've said on the telephone? Listen, you asshole, I'm not here to help you chase down old girlfriends—you've just made me late for a dinner party." I'd seen it in the newspaper. A gala event at the yacht club to grease the skids on Birk's bid for governor. Several well-known politicians from around the Southeast were slated to appear, and there would be drinks and dancing.

Birk's black tuxedo sucked up the light from his security lamps, and his daughter was in a gown. The boyfriend was wearing one of those long black coats that cost a lot of money and make tall people look short.

"Do you know why I've paid your way these last couple of years, you piece of shit?" Birk said. "And don't you dare forget it's been me lining your pockets. Do you really think you're worth the money I give you? Shit, you make me sick.

"I felt sorry for you." He held out his hands, palms up. "I'm one of the people who thought maybe you didn't bump off your girlfriend, but maybe I was wrong about that too." Birk was getting madder as he talked.

"Listen to me, you lousy fuck." He dropped his voice to a menacing whisper. "You just fell off the gravy train. You think you can sneak around my home and scare my little girl to death and play Dick Tracy with me and I'm gonna roll over and put my feet in the air?" There was a long menacing silence. He was looking at my face, but his eyes seemed unfocused.

" 'Tell you what I'm gonna do. I'll give you two minutes to get the fuck off my land and then I'm gonna send Seesee after you." He nodded to the side, and I looked to the corner of the patio. There, as large as a garbage can and still as a table leg, was as ugly a Rottweiler as I had ever seen. Birk had gone through a lot of dogs in the three years I'd been around him, but I had never seen one like this. I didn't spend a lot of time admiring the dog. Before my mind fully registered the fact that something that big was being held back by a choke chain the size

[45]

of my little finger, my body had turned and my feet were searching down the long driveway for the open gate.

The rich daughter saved my life, but I credit the mother's genes. I was almost at the gate when I heard her say, in a mixture of horror and fascination, "Daddy!"

Because of that, I heard the tiny, chinking sound of the choke chain being released and I took off in a dead run for my car. As I ran around to the driver's side, I could hear the dog's paws slapping the pavement behind me. I tore open the door and leapt inside, slamming it shut only to notice, just as the dog lunged, that the window was rolled down.

I fell to the side as the dog's chest crashed against the door, his teeth clacking together so close to my face that I could smell his breath. He fell back to the street and I sat up, fumbling for the window crank as he leapt again. I had the window about a quarter of the way up and he pushed his head inside, growling as his teeth clamped down on the thin collar of my dress coat. I pulled back on the crank and felt pressure as the window met the dog, gripping the puny alloy in both hands and drawing it back like an oar. The glass pressed into the dog's throat, but he didn't seem to notice until he tried to pull his head back for a better grip and found himself held. He tried to turn his head from side to side on the massive neck, but I kept pulling, watching the top of the window sink deeper into the thick folds of skin. Suddenly, he realized he was in trouble and tried to retreat, grunting as he twisted against the headliner, his claws tearing at the paint, screeching down to the metal.

I hung on to the crank desperately, hoping it wouldn't break off in my hands, and the dog went wild. He let go of my collar and clamped his mouth shut, eyes closed as he began thrashing against the window. He struggled. I heard the window crack and saw a spider web of lines form in the depths of the safety glass as he pushed and pulled. I put all my strength into the crank, giving up the notion of waiting him out, and it slipped over the metal nipple that held it. I had to lean into the door to get a better grip, and we touched heads. He was whimpering, and I could smell the stink of his fear. I pushed hard with my feet against the floorboard, my palms sweaty as I struggled to hold on to the crank.

The dog shuddered and his lips went slack. He blew out bubbles of blood that dotted the dash and fell on my jacket, moaned so deep inside him that it sounded as if it came from down the street, and died. His body sagged against the door and the window gave way, breaking out and holding its shape for a moment as the dog hung there, then falling outward as the massive body dropped to the street.

My arms were twitching as though they were attached to electric wires, but I managed to open the door and push the body aside until I could climb out. I heard the clapping of shoes on the drive as they ran to the sound of the commotion, and I reached down, wrapping my fingers around the dog's throat. I used up all my remaining strength lifting the carcass and walked on wobbly legs to the sidewalk. As Birk and the boyfriend rounded the corner from the large brick and cast-iron gate to the street, I pressed my thumbs into the dog's neck and shook it a few times for effect. I looked up at their comic forms, frozen in midstride, snarled, and dropped the lifeless body at my feet.

I turned my back on them and walked around the car's trunk to the door, stepped inside, and drove away with the window hanging like a thick cloth over the mutilated paint job. Better to leave them guessing.

I knew I had crossed the line then. For the first time in nearly five years, I had become a threat to someone. I saw it in Birk's eyes when he blinked. I heard it in his voice, and when he responded to Candy's name by mentioning old girlfriends, I knew it was real. There was something in his voice, in his eyes. It wasn't much to base a suspicion on, but I didn't need much. Up until then, though, I had wanted to be wrong.

SEVEN

"You did what?" Mark Thornton shouted at me over his office phone in his best lawyer voice.

"I killed his dog." I tried to make it sound like the sort of thing anyone would have done. We breathed at each other through the wires.

"Goddamn it, Mac," he said. "Are you out of your mind?"

"No," I said. "The dog started it."

"Shit," he said, then I heard rinky-tinky music and knew he'd put me on hold. I studied my drapes until he came back on the line.

"Okay, meet me at the marina at two-thirty." He hung up, and I did the same. I looked at my watch and it was only eleven o'clock. I'd gone into Palmetto Bay earlier that morning to order a new window for my car, and on the hunch that Birk would suspect I was setting him up for political blackmail, I stopped in at each of the other gubernatorial candidates' new offices and dawdled around inside long enough to give ulcers to whoever was following me around, or at least to the ones they reported to. I was sure somebody was following me.

I picked up the piece of white paper I had placed beside the phone and walked into the bathroom, staring at the series of numbers on it. I sat on the toilet seat and leaned back to think. Each movement made my shiner throb and my eye water. The boyfriend's roundhouse right had landed squarely on the side of my face, and if I had stayed on my feet he would have beaten me to a pulp. Lucky for me, I have a glass jaw. I really was lucky, though. He'd caught me on the grounds on the way out, not before I had broken in, and not, thank God, while I was inside the house in Birk's den with my fingers in his desk.

I wasn't surprised that the combination to Birk's safe was unchanged. He was so sure no one would attempt to cross him that I doubt he'd even thought about it. Besides, he'd have to learn new numbers if he did that. What I found in the safe, a built-in that occupied the lower right half of his giant desk, did surprise me. He

[48]

always kept his most important business in there. Stacks of contracts and bundles of cash for the little ceremonies he held on occasion to give "bonuses" to his "helpers." I'd watched him open the safe so many times that it was easy to remember the combination. This time, though, there was only one piece of paper lying on the thick floor of the safe. A sheet of paper with four sets of numbers scrawled on it, and nothing else. I'd ripped a sheet from his notepad and copied the numbers down before I closed the safe, but looking at them now for maybe the hundredth time, I still had no idea what they meant or why they were so important. A line of four four-digit numbers with no other markings anywhere.

I sat on the toilet seat and stared at the numbers. Sheevers's presence filled the room, and I waited for her to say "Oh. yeah. I know what those are," but there was only the sound of the wind in the trees outside.

I really hadn't expected to find anything in Birk's safe to implicate him in Candy Furay's rape and subsequent abortion, but I was ready to settle for any scrap of information that would let me know something he didn't want known. Now that I had it, I was still ignorant. I tried to imagine what the numbers might be; maybe the last four numbers of a telephone, or stock certificates, auto tag numbers, or any damned thing under the sun. Finally, frustrated, I stood and stuffed the paper into my shirt.

Nothing seemed right. Nicaraguan Contras didn't need to be on private land, and Birk was much too careful and powerful to risk everything by raping a fourteen-year-old girl. I paced the house like a raccoon in a cage and chased my mind down one dead end after another. All my notes on Tommy Lovett and the Sunset Girls had been removed from my house and car those three days I spent in jail, but I have a very good memory for details. Sheevers was murdered about two months after the Limestone Creek killings, and if Candace had waited until she knew she was pregnant before she told her mother, I'd have to add at least two months to that. She would have waited until she was sure. I needed to find out exactly when it happened.

My coffee table was a mosaic of notes and diagrams that reminded me of the past. The litter of my investigation overflowed onto the floor. In the weeks since Katherine had gone home I'd been working on my jigsaw puzzle of facts, but there were too many pieces still missing. Unlike a store-bought puzzle, there was no picture on the box to go by. I had gone through the courthouse records and the library for any scraps of information on our public figures and the makeup of Omni,

[49]

BELLAIRE PUBLIC LIBRARY
BELLAIRE, OHIO
92-4285

Inc., but there was precious little to be culled. My contacts around town had been silent, but I hoped that would change abruptly after my visit to Birk's house the night before. Birk wouldn't take chances now that he had his one big shot to become governor, but he couldn't let me get away with what I'd done, either.

I stood over the coffee table and took a last look at all the parts, then leaned down and scooped them up, making sure I got every scrap. I dumped them into a paper bag, rolled it closed, and tossed it into the garbage. The telephone rang and I debated answering it, but there was no need to put anything off now. The ball was in play.

"Hello," I said into the phone.

"Hey, Mac." Katherine's voice was relaxed. I sat on the arm of the sofa and closed my eyes. "I've been thinking about you," she said.

We hadn't talked since she left, and I had just about convinced myself she was only a client, never mind that I'd forgotten to mention money to her the entire time. Never mind my trip to the bank to withdraw my own money to help her get away from Las Vegas. It wouldn't take many clients like her to have me resettled at the Mission, fighting for a place in the soup line.

"Are you okay?" she said.

"Yeah," I said. "But you're not a secret here anymore. I confronted Birk last night, and when I asked if he'd ever heard of Candace Furay, he made a puddle." I waited for it to sink in.

"Okay." Suddenly, I was afraid she was somewhere close, somewhere exposed.

"Where are you?" I said.

"I'm at Dr. Kuyatt's office. We got an early start this morning so I can get as much together about Candy as possible. Mark Thornton called last night and booked me on a flight to Tallahassee this afternoon so I can make the deposition." I heard a man talking in the background, and there was a pause before Katherine spoke again. "Dr. Kuyatt wants me to ask you a few questions before I hang up." She giggled, and it sounded nasty. "Mr. Thornton said he tried to call you last night but you weren't home."

"I have a meeting with him in a couple of hours," I said. "I'm sure he'll fill me in. Do you have to come back to do it?" I wanted her as far away as possible. "Can't you go to a lawyer there and have it faxed to Mark?"

"Yes, I guess so." She sounded disappointed. "Mr. Thornton wanted me to come there so I could deal with his people, and I thought maybe you could drive over for dinner or something."

I took a deep breath and scratched my chest. Even as I thought that I really did have to take her the getaway money, I knew that I was climbing out on that little limb again. "I only go to restaurants that have drive-through windows."

"That's fine," she said, and again I heard a man talking. Katherine said something to him and then came back on the line. "Mac, Dr. Kuyatt wants to know if you handle stress well." I looked out the screen door to my car, the door mutilated.

"Pretty well," I said. She laughed in my ear and sounded happy. "I think he's worried about you taking advantage of me," she said. "He's afraid you'll go macho."

"That won't happen," I said. "Tell him that I'm really just a woman trapped in a man's body, but it's okay because I'm a lesbian." She covered the phone, and I heard muffled conversation.

"He didn't think that was funny," Katherine said. "But I'd like to hear more about it." She was in a good mood and I wanted to be with her. "Say you'll be there."

"I'll be there," I repeated. "Where?"

"Ask Mark Thornton. He's made all the plans. All I know is, I'll arrive at six o'clock this afternoon, your time. Can you pick me up at the airport?"

"No way," I said. "I've seen how you act in airports." I remembered my appointment with Phil's Glass Shop for the afternoon. "I really won't be able to meet you there," I said. "But I'll find out from Mark where you'll be staying and pick you up for dinner."

"I'll be ready." Again there was conversation on her end. "I'd better get off the line," she said. "We have a lot of paperwork to finish, and my plane leaves soon."

"See you tonight," I said, and hung up. I liked Katherine and enjoyed her company, but there was no room in my life for this kind of relationship. She never really said whether she was married or not, but I was, in a ceremony of blood and sacrifice, and I knew Sheevers waited patiently for me. She wasn't angry at me for letting them kill her, she was simply waiting for the day when I would join her—a Wagnerian ending where she would cradle my wide-eyed soul in hers and take me to the promised land. But first I had to finish this thing that had been thrust on me, to keep my oath to Patty's friend.

I fiddled around the house, fixing things that I'd been putting off as I waited for two-thirty. I left early and drove around Palmetto Bay. It really was a beautiful place, built before the turn of the century by a coalition of shipbuilders and timbermen when labor was cheap and men were desperate for work. The choice locations were still show-cases of giant homes with pillared fronts and glassed-in views of the magnificent Gulf of Mexico.

Downtown Palmetto Bay was laid out to run parallel to the bay and ended at a marina dominated by a large railroad station that had been converted to government offices and fancy retail shops. Sleek white sailboats with blue sail covers were nudging out the old fishing boats, and shrimpers were sinking under the weight of accumulated regulations. Parking lots were connected by access roads around the shops, and I pulled into a space with a view of the water. Seagulls stood on the steel handrails with their backs to the wind and waited impatiently for scraps of food. I glanced around and decided the two guys in a green Dodge truck were my keepers.

I leaned over the wheel and let the breeze dry out the back of my shirt. A reggae blues song on the radio added a soundtrack to a large ship that crept along the distorted blue horizon. Mark's cream-colored Mercedes slipped silently around the nose of my car and eased to a stop. His window was in line with mine. Mark was one of those people born to be a lawyer, and as he sat looking over the parking lot, I tried to imagine him as a baby in a crib, hair styled and eyebrow arched, already possessing a mouth full of perfect white teeth. His clothes were immaculate and his skin tone perfect. He worshiped at "Our Lady of the Perpetual Tan." I'd known him for over seven years, and looking at him now, I wondered if there was a painting of him, in his home, that showed him aging normally.

"The clowns in the green truck?" he spoke at last.

"Yeah," I said. "I think so."

"Mac, I don't know if you're my substitute for a life of crime," he said, "but I want you to listen to me now. If you interrupt even once, I'm leaving and you can try hiring a lawyer who might want to be paid every once in a while." He paused, but I wasn't about to say anything.

"I like you, but that doesn't mean shit. You've just challenged one of the most powerful men in Florida to a fight, and the odds of you winning are practically nonexistent. Even with the testimony of Ms. Furay and her daughter.

"I talked to Katherine last night and she's coming to Tallahassee to give a deposition to my staff. She's bringing one from Candace and some transcripts from her doctor." His car was so quiet I couldn't tell if it was running, but I figured it was because the air conditioner was blowing at him hard enough for me to feel the coolness in my open window. He noticed my door.

"Holy God!" he whispered to me. "The dog did that?"

I thought it was possible he was trying to trick me into talking out of turn, so I just nodded.

"Mac, I want you to know I'm scared shitless going up against these guys. It's taken a long time for me to get a foothold in Palmetto Bay, and I don't want to blow it." He leaned toward me. "But I believe in you, and after talking to Katherine Furay, I believe her, too. But this is the big time, and you're going to have to act responsibly. From now on I don't even want a little trouble—in fact, if Bob Birk pisses in your soup I want you to say thank you, do you understand?" I nodded again.

"You can talk now, goddamn it!"

"Okay," I said. "Where's Katherine staying tonight? I'm taking her to dinner." Mark's face got hard, and each time he clenched his jaw his ears wiggled. He spoke through his teeth.

"This is not a fucking game, Mac!" he was really mad. "If you think it is, then you can save us both a lot of trouble by dropping this whole thing right now and leaving me alone. Once I file it I can't turn back, and I'm going to make some enemies here. That doesn't make me happy."

"I'm not an idiot, Mark," I said. "And I'm not going to take unnecessary chances. But Katherine doesn't know anybody here but me, and I'm going to keep an eye on her."

"What about them?" Mark nodded toward the truck.

"They won't be with me for long." Mark studied my face, then scribbled on a sheet of paper and handed it to me. It said, "Bainbridge Motor Lodge on Tennessee. Room 303."

I put the note in my shirt pocket with the other sheet of paper. "Be careful, Mac," he said. "After we get the deposition in the morning she'll be safer, but all hell's going to break loose when the press gets hold of this."

"Thanks, Mark." He smiled at me and put his car in gear, slipping away with no good-bye. I stared at the water for a while, then, pretending I didn't see them, I drove past the truck and headed across town to Phil's Glass. I left my car with a man named Teddy and sat in the air-conditioned waiting room, thumbing through health-and-fitness magazines until I found a week-old Tallahassee newspaper in a stack of others from Pensacola and Gainesville. One copy of the *Palmetto Bay Sun* lay on an end table and was soaked in coffee from a leaking Styrofoam cup. Three saturated cigarette filters bobbed in the leftover coffee. I was pretty familiar with the capital, but I thought it might be a good idea to check restaurant ads and decide where we'd go. I looked

[53]

through the plate-glass window and they were already removing the inside lining of my door.

I was pulling the newspaper apart in sections, looking for an eats column, when an article caught my eye. At first I didn't know why, and I almost tossed it aside. Then I saw the headline and felt a piece fall into place. It was a short editorial on battling drugs, and it mentioned a tough new enforcement bill introduced to the legislature as HR4512.

I reached into my pocket and pulled out the larger, folded piece of paper, opening it as I let the newspaper settle in my lap. The third series of numbers on the sheet of notepaper, the one I had copied from Birk's safe, was 4512. I looked back and forth from the article to the paper a couple of times, then refolded the page and put it back into my pocket.

I read the article and all it said was that the bill had been designed to help "law enforcement" in its battle against drugs by clarifying older laws on the confiscation of property. I finished reading without learning much more than that. The article was either poorly written or intentionally vague.

It seemed the numbers may have been just four "get tough" laws for Birk to use so he could sound like a legitimate candidate. But why hide them in a safe? I was getting pretty fed up with being stupid, so I found a pay phone and made a collect call to Mel Shiver.

He still wasn't very friendly, but when I told him about the numbers and the article in the newspaper he came alive. He milked me for all the information I had, asked how Katherine was, and said he'd let me know if he found out anything. Teddy was waving at me through the window, and he looked pleased. I stepped into the heat and he handed me the bill. He wiped his face with a brown cloth.

"Boy, Mr. Clay, that window was a mess!" he said.

"Did you fix it?" I asked.

"Oh, yeah," he said, his curiosity kicking the crap out of his manners until he broke down. "How in the world did it happen?"

"Raccoons," I said. "At the state park. I left a loaf of bread on the seat when I went swimming." I shook my head slowly. "I won't make that mistake again." I wrote a check and gave it to Teddy, a man with a newfound respect for the wild kingdom.

The afternoon limped along. I cleaned up and checked my wallet for cash. My clothes felt as if they fit wrong and my hair bounced back up when I tried to brush it down. It felt like prom night, and I expected zits to begin popping out on my cheeks.

[54]

Plato and Aristotle sat in the green pickup truck, a cartoon of tubular bumpers covered with Bocephus stickers, worn balloon tires, and a black roll bar that had floodlights perched on it like crows on a fence. They were trying to be unobtrusive, and it was hard as hell to act as though I didn't notice them.

I drove toward the interstate, glancing at my watch to make sure it was still rush hour. The traffic was heavy but had smoothed out a bit by the time I whipped my car into the outside lane. I checked the mirror and saw my pals make a space for themselves several car lengths back. I accelerated to match the flow and turned on the radio, catching the last hour of the Red Flannery program, a petulant diatribe about ethics and morals in American business. Broadcasting live from a satellite pickup network in Mobile, Alabama, he was the commuter's friend, stroking their helpless anger and encouraging them to write to their congressmen about pornography, graft, and corruption. I still couldn't believe he and Mel Shiver were old friends.

I flipped on my turn signal, braked hard, and pulled onto the emergency strip, watching the green truck slow down and pull over behind me a couple of hundred yards back. I got out of my car and walked to the front, leaned down and looked at my tire, scratched my head, hopped back in, and darted back into traffic. I punched it up to speed again and watched in the mirror as the guys in the truck finally found a hole and raced back onto the road. They had lost a lot of ground and pulled into the fast lane to catch up.

As soon as I saw them merge into the other lane I put on my blinker and pulled over again. I didn't look at them as they zipped by, but as soon as they found a place to pull off the road I put my foot to the floor, sliced out a thin strip of asphalt between two eighteen-wheelers, and hit the passing lane at warp speed. When I swerved onto the exit ramp they were nowhere in sight. I drove under the interstate and took the eastbound lane to Tallahassee.

EIGHT

I stopped in the parking lot of the Bainbridge Motor Lodge but didn't get out of my car. The lights on the third-floor balcony were bright, and the door to Katherine's room was just sitting there, waiting to be opened. My nerves were shot. I looked back with longing to a couple of weeks before when I was comfortable in my own little gutter, biding my time and waiting for judgment day. I didn't want to get involved with anyone and, even if I did, why did it have to be someone with these kinds of problems? I reached for the handle but didn't pull it, couldn't act. Two men got out of a Camaro that was parked in a corner space and walked toward the motel, and I thought, *Those guys can get out of their car, why can't I get out of mine?* Then I recognized the taller of the two.

I hadn't seen Allen Farmer for almost three years, but his walk, his profile were enough to turn my stomach. He free-lanced for Birk on occasion, when one of Bob's associates needed something really lousy done, and as soon as I saw him, I knew why he was there. He and the other man, small and wiry, had passed into the shadows of the first-floor landing and were moving quickly. I almost tore my door off its hinges getting out, and I could see them rounding the second landing as I ran across the pavement. It didn't seem as if I was gaining on them at all.

I spun on the landing and raced up the steps to the second floor, and when I twisted up the next flight of steps I tore a red fire extinguisher from its platform, tucked it under my arm, and tried to fly up the last incline. From the third floor I could hear the sounds of a door crashing open.

I rounded the corner just as the second man disappeared into the room. When I cleared the open doorway I saw Katherine backed against the far wall and knew there was nothing I could do. Farmer was a good five steps ahead of me, and, still on the run, he pulled a large automatic pistol from his belt and raised it to Katherine's face. I expected her to fall back and cover up, but she did the opposite. She stepped toward Allen and grabbed his wrist, then twisted back, hooking his leg as he raced by. His pistol fired and the slug hit the wall just a fraction of a second before his face slammed into it, a little above the bullet hole.

The second man took a wild swing and his fist connected with Katherine's jaw as she was trying to regain her balance. She fell back and crashed into Allen as I brought the fire extinguisher around in a wide arc. It crunched into the smaller man's rib cage just under his arm, and he dropped like a brick. I drew back to hit him again, when I heard Katherine yell.

I couldn't believe it, but Farmer, after sliding down the wall, was coming back up again and the gun was still in his hand. Katherine put one hand flat against the wall and kicked hard, her foot slapping into his throat. He turned to stare at her with a dopey look on his face as I brought the extinguisher down on his forehead. It broke the skin just above his left eye, and he crumbled onto the carpet, blood pouring across his nose. The gun clattered over the nightstand and dropped at my feet. When I bent to retrieve it the small man came to life. He jumped forward and threw a body block into Katherine, knocking her onto the bed, then came at me, his eyes wild and mean. When he slammed into me I brought my fist around and got in one clean shot, catching him in the eye. He careened into the wall, bounced off, and ran to the door as I raised the pistol. He must have been in a panic, confused and dazed, because he ran onto the balcony and leapt over the railing as though it were a low hedge. I heard a woman scream from three floors below.

Katherine struggled to a sitting position on the edge of the bed, and was staring at Farmer when I sat down beside her. She had a curious smile on her face, and I knew she was close to slipping into shock. She drew away when I touched her arm, but I said her name and she looked at me, looked at the smashed door, and called me Mc-Donald. She wrapped her arms around my waist and held on tight. I heard people shouting in the parking lot and, in the distance, sirens screamed.

A glance at Farmer was enough to see he wouldn't make another miraculous resurrection, so I leaned down, still in Katherine's grasp, and placed the pistol on the carpet. I pushed it away from me with my foot. The police would be in the motel room in a minute, and cops don't like civilians with guns. I stroked Katherine's back and pulled away to study her face. Her eyes were a little glassy, but she was working on her breathing and seemed to be leveling off. I knew I should try to get her to talk, to take a personal inventory. Her jaw was swelling and turning purple.

"What was that?" I asked. "Karate?"

She shook her head. "No, it's judo. I'm not very good at it."

I nodded at Farmer. "Don't tell him that, it'll just embarrass him." She almost smiled. "You were great," I said. "I mean it, you were fantastic."

"Thank God you came, Mac," she said. It sounded as if an army was storming the third floor, and I told Katherine to be still. They came into the room with guns ready, eyes alert. They were well trained, and I relaxed a little. Good, professional cops make few mistakes in this kind of situation. We waited silently until they checked out the room, and I could hear other motel patrons being escorted down the stairs. One cop picked up the pistol by the barrel and another took it away. The first called for an ambulance as another policeman checked Farmer for a pulse.

They told us to stand up and move away from each other, and after the first cop checked us for weapons, he placed two fingers gently on Katherine's chin and asked if she'd like to sit down. She nodded gratefully and, clutching my elbow, sat on the bed. I draped an arm over her shoulder and she leaned against me.

Katherine started to tell him how it happened, how they broke her door down, but he held up a hand. All pistols were holstered. "Yes, ma'am," he said. "But please wait until the lieutenant gets here so you only have to tell the whole story once." He was kind and polite to her, and he practically broadcasted the feeling that everything was under control. I liked this guy.

The lieutenant finally arrived. He was a large, sloppy man with no taste in clothes. Before he entered the room he leaned over the railing, hands in pockets, looked down, and said, "Oh, yuck." He stuck his head in the splintered doorway.

"Somebody drain the pool?" he said, and I heard a cop laugh. Paramedics rushed past him and removed Allen Farmer.

It took almost an hour to tell the story, and by then Mark Thornton had pushed his way into the room with two angry women who whisked Katherine away with a nod of approval from the lieutenant. That left him alone with Mark and me. When I told the lieutenant earlier that I was a private detective, he rolled his eyes and said, "Jesus H. Christ."

I asked Mark where they had taken Katherine, and he told me she was under his protection until he could take her deposition in the morning and he wasn't going to tell anyone where that was. "Who did you tell about this place, goddamn it," I said.

"What are you talking about?" Mark bristled. "Those two men must have followed you over here."

"No way," I said. The lieutenant stood between us. "They were already in the parking lot when I pulled in." I glanced at the cop. "I watched them get out of their car and they didn't even know I was here."

"You know which car is theirs?" The lieutenant was interested, so I told him and he sauntered out the door.

"Damn you, Mac," Mark whispered through clenched teeth. I told you, 'no trouble'!"

"Hey," I said. "There wouldn't have been any trouble if I hadn't shown up—they would've just blown her head off and grabbed a burger on the way home, you dumb shit. I want to know where Katherine is right now, Mark." I looked around the room, Katherine's open suitcase pushed to one side of the double bed, Farmer's blood splattered along the beige carpet and white wall. A pair of low heels had been kicked across the room, one almost crushed behind the broken door. I walked to the door and picked up Katherine's shoes.

"These guys knew right where to find her—think about it," I said. "They got out of their car and came straight to this room, and somebody told them how to get here."

Mark Thornton paled as it finally sank in. His odds of catching Bob Birk by surprise had disappeared. Somewhere along the links of procedure Mark had been following, his information had been intercepted. Birk knew everything he knew. I was thankful I hadn't told Mark about anything except the rape of Katherine Furay's daughter. I had planned to fill him in on the other, more serious charges after he'd taken the depositions; after he had committed himself.

"Holy God," he said. He gripped the chair behind him for support, pulled it from under the desk, and sat down. He put a shaking hand over his eyes. I kept thinking how quick and brutal this was, even for Bob Birk.

"Mac, I'm sorry," Mark said. "I swear to you I'll find out who's responsible for this . . . this crime. Jesus, they tried to kill her."

"I want to go there, Mark," I said. "Now. You're going to take me to Katherine and you're going to pull whatever strings it takes to get her deposition on record tonight." He dropped the hand and looked up at me. I took his arm and lifted him to his feet. "Then we're going to

[59]

take her to the airport and put her on a plane to Las Vegas. She'll have a police escort all the way."

The lieutenant had drifted back in as we talked, and I explained what I knew. Mark told him where he'd sent Katherine. He stepped out of the room again, and I could hear conversation at the stairwell. He came back and said we could follow him there. As we left the room he handed me a card with his name and phone number on it. "Thanks for not being a dick," he said.

Tallahassee had never been so big and traffic had never moved more slowly than when we followed Lieutenant Lonnie Patrick to the small motel where Katherine sat safely at a table in a cramped, knotty-pine kitchenette. I told Mark Thornton the rest of Katherine's story on the ride over, and he was still in shock when we arrived. Katherine's face was swollen and there was a rip in the side of her dark-red dress. She stood up when we came in and wrapped an arm loosely around my waist. I handed her the pair of shoes. Mark headed for the telephone.

"I know this is a stupid question," I said, "but are you all right?"

Katherine nodded slowly and put her other hand to her neck. "Yes," she said, "I think so, but I've never really known what fear was until tonight. I can't stop thinking about it."

"That's natural," Lieutenant Patrick said casually. "I'm just surprised a good-looking woman like you isn't used to having men breaking down your door."

Katherine smiled at him. "Usually they don't want to kill me until after they get to know me."

He laughed. "By the way," he said, "nobody thought to have you examined at the motel room, so I asked the paramedics to stop by later and take a look at you. They can probably give you something to take the pain away. That jaw has to be hurting you."

"Thank you, Lieutenant," Katherine said. She was having trouble talking. "That was nice."

A knock on the door brought every head around, and Lieutenant Patrick opened it. Two men stood sleepily in the doorway, laptop computers and briefcases clutched tightly against their chests. Mark called out to them, "Perry! Cain? Come on in!" He explained to the rest of us that he was having people come out from town to take the deposition, and he asked Lieutenant Patrick whom he should contact to have Katherine's things brought over from the Bainbridge Motor Lodge.

"I'll take care of it," Patrick said. He stepped around the men and waved me over. I squeezed Katherine's shoulders lightly and walked across the room to the lieutenant. "Why don't you step outside with me for a minute," he said politely, nodding to Katherine as he left the room. I shrugged.

"Okay." I looked back at her and thumbed toward the parking lot. "I'll be back," I said. The lieutenant stopped and turned to me when we reached his car.

"Are you going to stay with her tonight?" he asked, and I said I didn't know. He raised an eyebrow. "Let me tell you something, Clay," he said. "I don't know what the hell's going on here—not really; but if I find out you're fucking with me, I'm not going to like it. In fact, I'll probably find a way to kick your ass, is that clear?"

"Back off, Lieutenant," I said. "If I ever learn what really happened tonight you'll be the first to know, and that's a promise. This is all way over my head." I leaned on his car. "I'd love to dump it on you."

I honestly wanted to tell him everything. It would have been a relief to get this case off my back. There was no way I could win against these odds. There were plenty more where Farmer and his pal came from, and Birk had access to all of them. We'd won at the motel earlier, but that had been pure luck and I don't believe in luck. Patrick bent down and reached into his car, made a couple of calls, and looked back at me.

"Gotta run," he said. "Maybe I'll see you later." He drove off and left me alone in the night. The motel sat on a hill south of downtown Tallahassee, and I stood under the trees watching the distant flow of traffic moving like rivers of light. Crisply dressed lawyers began arriving with their aides, and were checked by a policeman before they slipped through the door to Katherine's new room. I thought of her and her courage, and about the long road ahead. She was alive because of chance. If I hadn't been there, if I hadn't recognized Farmer. If Katherine Furay hadn't been so damned brave.

I sat on a grassy hill beneath a thick-trunked oak and sank into my mind. I knew we would never make it unless I could find a path to follow, some plan to overcome those tremendous odds. Most people, especially in my profession, like to think of everything in their lives as David against Goliath, but in reality most are just David versus another David. And the advantage is usually on our side, because we're calling the shots. Now, however, I really was facing a Goliath, and the size differences were evident. It would take more than blind luck and some bold moves on my part to stay in the game. I searched deeper into the maze of facts, looking for some key to the solution, but found nothing but high walls and deep holes.

[61]

Finally, unable to go on, I came back to the surface. I opened my eyes and saw Lieutenant Patrick sitting on the trunk of his car, a cigarette dangling between his lips. His eyes were on me. "How long have you been there?" I said. Instead of answering he took a long drag on his cigarette, then flipped it out into the dark parking lot. The sparks scattered in a gust of wind.

"When I was in the Vietnamese Highlands, a little smudge called Tan Canh, there was this guy who used to do that before he went down into the tunnels. I never saw him, but I heard about him. Everyone said he was the best." For the first time in years, I wished I had a cigarette.

"Are you a veteran?" he asked. I nodded.

"But I don't have any war stories," I said.

"That's okay," the lieutenant said. "I have a couple more."

I could see people moving around in the motel room, and I imagined the smell of coffee. "This guy got separated from his outfit around Rocket Ridge in 'seventy-two. They were hauling ass to the south and Charlie hit them hard. A few guys made it back, but nobody expected to see him again. He showed up at a field hospital over a week later with a broken leg and two bullets in his side, and they patched him up and sent him home." Lieutenant Patrick slid off the trunk and leaned against the car. He lit another cigarette. "Someone said he went to Florida."

"Golly!" I said. "What do you suppose happened to him?"

"Who knows," Patrick said. "Want some coffee?"

I looked to the busy motel room and back at him. "You bet," I said.

We drove to the Waffle House and took a table away from the door. He ordered coffee and we watched people come and go. "Are you always this friendly on a first date?" I said.

"I still don't know what's going on here," he said. "But you're in trouble up to your neck. Maybe higher." A heavyset man walked wearily through the door, followed by a pale woman in rumpled clothes. The man pulled at the seat of his pants. They sat together on the stools and groaned. Lonnie Patrick smiled at the man, then turned back to me.

"I'll tell you something you might not know." He leaned over the table toward me. "You're not the only one who knows about Bob Birk. Even over here we know what he's capable of, given the need. But this doesn't make sense, Clay." The big cop shook his head. "That wasn't retaliation tonight, no matter what the woman did to him. It's mur-

[62]

der—cold-blooded murder—and it makes me wonder who's pulling the strings."

"What do you mean?" I asked, trying not to read too much into it.

"C'mon, Clay." He sounded disgusted. "Birk's playing for it all, and you know it. And you didn't just stumble in off the streets in time to save Ms. Furay, so spare me the shit.

"I had a check run on you. I know who you are; and I know about your girlfriend in Palmetto Bay. I remember when it happened."

"Do you?" I said. "What do you remember, Lieutenant, that she was killed by a prowler or that she was murdered to get me off the case I was working on?"

"Either way," he said, "you must be feeling a little snake-bit right now."

"What about that, Lieutenant? Do you think those two men were there tonight to steal Katherine's traveler's checks?" I was tired of being shoved.

"I don't know," he said, staying casual. "Tell me."

"I wish I could," I said. "But right now I don't know enough to make sense of it. Believe me, if I could give this whole thing to you, I would." Calls on his portable radio hadn't stopped since we sat down, and it became just another background noise, like the shouting of young couples at the other tables and the tired hacking of the weary man on the stool. A motorcycle roared by in the darkness outside. We drank more coffee.

Patrick got to his feet and paid the bill. I dropped a dollar on the table and followed him to his car. When we arrived at the motel, I climbed out and he turned down his radio. "You ever wonder if maybe Vietnam never happened? That maybe you just imagined it?"

"Sometimes," I said.

"Now that I'm getting older, I'm thinking all kinds of weird shit like that," Patrick said. "Can you imagine the retirement homes they're going to have to build for us? A bunch of paranoid old bastards." He chuckled. "They won't have to give us rooms, just a little dark bunker with a flashlight and a gun." I looked into his face for a sign of humor, but there wasn't any. He put the car in gear and gave me a mock salute. "I'll have someone here in the morning to escort Ms. Furay to the airport." He pulled away slowly but kept talking. "Don't lose my fucking card." I slapped the rear fender of his car as he went by.

"You're not alone, Clay," he said. "Don't forget that."

* * *

[63]

Most of the people had gone home, and the room was a trash pile of computer paper, Styrofoam coffee cups, and empty doughnut boxes. Mark was talking on the phone and the two women sat with an older, distinguished man who wore a styled, silver beard. The bathroom door opened, and Katherine stepped out holding a wet towel to her face. She was in loose, dark-green slacks, a white blouse, and tennis shoes. Her suitcase sat on the narrow dresser. She looked up from the towel and smiled at me.

"I hoped you'd come back." She slurred her words.

"I said I would." I watched her drift languidly toward the bed. She laughed.

"I know," she said. "But I just took some pills a doctor sent over and I don't want to be alone." Mark looked up from the table and cupped a hand over the phone.

"You won't be," he said to Katherine. "Lydia and Francis are going to stay with you."

"You want to bet?" Katherine said, holding out a hand to the two women. "No offense, ladies, but I want everyone out of here. Now." Mark mumbled into the phone and hung up. The women exchanged glances with the man with the silver beard. Katherine sighed and sat on the edge of the bed.

"I'm very tired," she said. "I've given you my life story and my face hurts. I have a cop at my door and Mac will be here with me, right?" She looked at me and I nodded.

Mark stood and whispered to the women. They wouldn't look at me but filed past Katherine, touching her on their way out the door. She thanked them. The older man stood and Mark introduced us.

"McDonald Clay," he said, nervous as a kid in a school play, "this is Mr. Robert Booth Holmes. I asked him to come tonight for this meeting because, frankly, this entire affair has escalated beyond my level of expertise." I shook hands with the legendary Tallahassee attorney. I figured the handshake alone cost me about three hundred dollars, and I got as nervous as Mark. Holmes and I grunted at each other, and he collected his briefcase.

"I'm going back to Palmetto Bay tonight," Mark said to me as he escorted Holmes to the door. "Are you taking Katherine to the airport tomorrow?"

I was winging it. "Sure," I said. "I should be home around noon, if you need me."

"It's going to hit the papers in the morning." Mark looked worried.

[64]

"I think there was even something on the news tonight, but I don't know what was said.

"We're on pretty shaky ground right now," he said. "Even with what happened here, there's still very little proof."

"What about Birk's get-out-of-town note?" I said.

"It's going to be analyzed," Mark said. "But even if it's Birk's handwriting, his attorneys can tear it apart."

Holmes looked impatient, and they left. I stepped out and watched them drive away, then told the young cop I'd be there for the night and he said, "Okay."

I went inside and closed the door behind me, checking the locks and windows before I sat down beside Katherine. Her eyelids were beginning to hang at half-mast over those beautiful green eyes. "I'm starved," she said.

"Want me to get you a milk shake?"

"No," she said, sounding too tired to talk. "Doctor said it wasn't broken—said I'll feel better tomorrow." Katherine put a hand on my arm and slid it down until she found my fingers. She squeezed. "I don't want to live my life like this, Mac," she said. "But we can't quit."

"We won't quit, Katherine, that's a promise." She dropped the towel from her other hand and groaned as she stood up.

"Pajamas," she said. She shuffled to the narrow dresser and pulled a gown from her suitcase draped it across her shoulder, and shuffled into the bathroom. I ambled across the room, drank a glass of tepid water from the tap, and turned down the bed covers.

I didn't hear the bathroom door open but turned at the rustle of her gown, and Katherine was in my arms, gently wrapped around me. Her hair tickled my chin. I eased her down on the cool sheets and her arms fell limp at her sides. I pulled the covers over her and kicked off my shoes, dragged up a comfortable chair, and sat down, stretching my legs. She pulled a hand from under the covers, and I held it as she slept. I heard the cops change shifts early in the morning.

NINE

"I want breakfast!" I opened my eyes and there was an angel in my face. In fact, the angel was in my lap, dressed in the same casual clothes from the night before. "I want it outdoors, and I want sunshine and a breeze." She kissed me, and this time there was no confusion. The softness of her lips lingered after she backed away.

"Mac, they're not going to take my life away from me," Katherine said. "I don't like being told what to do, and I hate the feeling of helplessness I had last night. You and I are going to eat out this morning on the way to my plane. We may even do a little shopping."

I smiled at her and pushed her off my lap. When I stood, my legs were stiff and my back was sore from swinging the fire extinguisher. My eye still hurt. "Boy, what I wouldn't give for ten minutes alone with a toothbrush."

Katherine turned to her suitcase and produced toothpaste and a brush. When I stepped out of the bathroom fifteen minutes later, blinking cold water from my eyes, Lieutenant Patrick was standing inside the front door with his arms crossed. Katherine had her back to me and didn't turn around when I closed the door.

"What's wrong?" I asked. Katherine didn't move. I followed Patrick's eyes to the bed where the newspaper held a large color photograph of a grinning Bob Birk. The caption read, "I knew they would try something . . ." I was tired of seeing his face. The headline said, "BIRK ACCUSED OF RAPE," but the front page was a series of articles on the contributions he'd made over the years to the people of Florida, tales of his selfless devotion to the "little guy." When I followed the instructions and turned to page 2A, I was startled by separate photographs of Katherine and me, mine taken sometime during my incarceration five years before. The glaze in my eyes made Charles Manson look like a cherub.

Someone had written short biographies of her and me, and we

[66]

both sounded pretty disgusting. I tried to imagine the time it would take to put together something like this and the power to place it on the front pages of a seemingly respectable newspaper. Fear tapped me on the shoulder and said, "Boo."

The quote under Birk's picture said he was expecting the opposition to come up with something to stop his fast climb to the front-runner position in the race for governor but he was surprised, not only by the charges, but by the two slimy characters they hired to pull it off. He mentioned that he had used me to do some work for him over the last few years because he thought it was possible I'd been given a raw deal on the murder charge, but that he'd fired me a couple of nights before after finding me trespassing on his property. He said his daughter told him I was "peeping" at her.

Birk said the one thing that didn't surprise him was the violence in Katherine's motel room. He said he'd seen Allen Farmer and me drinking together recently and speculated that what happened was the result of a lover's triangle. I had to sit down.

This was good stuff, the best I'd ever seen. Whoever was running Birk's campaign seemed to have unlimited access to power and money, and I honestly felt like crawling in a hole. The printed story of his raping Candace at the Sunset Hotel made Katherine sound like a pimp and her daughter a whore. The hotel came out as the Vatican and Birk as the pope. They made sure to give Tommy Lovett the position of injured cardinal. Birk must have called his handlers right after I left his house, but I still couldn't imagine how they'd done such a complete job of burying us.

"If you plan on getting your butts out of this," the lieutenant said, "you'd better not waste time sitting on them."

I looked over at him and at Katherine. She turned from the window and laughed. "Lieutenant Patrick," she hooked her arm in his and held out her hand to me, "why don't you join us for breakfast?"

"Will you tell me what's happening here?" he asked.

"All of it," I said. I stood up and tossed the paper into the trash can. "Let's eat."

We spent over an hour in a restaurant having breakfast as people stared. Katherine and I took turns filling in the story as Patrick sat, spellbound.

"What're you going to do about it?" he asked. I shrugged. He exhaled. Katherine ate.

She wanted to call home and brace Candy for the news, so we left

[67]

her at a pay phone in the airport and stood together at a window. "I have to tell you, Clay," Patrick said, "my natural inclination is to put a lot of space between you and me. Cops are territorial and pretty damned loyal, actually. We're the pit bulls of the human race. You don't live here, so I could turn my back on you, but Tallahassee is my town and this guy Birk is starting to make the hair on my neck stand up.

"I don't know how he's connected, but this ain't ordinary." He looked uncomfortable with his candid monologue. "Truthfully, Ms. Furay's story sounds like a crock of shit to me. Like some kind of radical junk from the sixties. That's what scares me, I think, because I know it's real." Someone shouted my name, and it startled me. When I turned, bright lights flashed in my eyes and I heard the lieutenant tell someone to back off.

I blinked my eyes and marveled at the explosions of yellow inside my eyelids. "Is it true you're a convicted murderer?" a man yelled.

"What?" I said.

"Or were you acquitted?" another said.

"Of what?"

"Murder," a woman said.

"I said back off!" Patrick shouted at the crowd.

"I've never been charged with murder," I said. I was surrounded by a mob of reporters, some with tape recorders, some with cameras and video equipment.

"Who paid you to implicate Bob Birk?" a male voice boomed.

"Who paid you to ask me that?" I said. Patrick grabbed my arm and changed places with me.

"C'mon, people, give the man some room," he said. "Stay cool," he whispered to me. People were trying to hold microphones up over his shoulder to reach my face. Floodlights were turned on. I thought about picking my nose.

"Hey!" I knew it was Katherine before I turned my head. As the press beat each other senseless trying to whip their stuff around and aim it at her, she stood defiant, and I heard Patrick say, "Shit." I wondered if he was as proud of her as I was.

"Bob Birk raped my daughter when she was fourteen years old, and a lot of it just came to light in therapy." Katherine was balanced and direct. "I came to Tallahassee yesterday to file a lawsuit against Birk, and two men broke down my door and tried to kill me. If Mr. Clay hadn't shown up just then to take me to the lawyers' office for my deposition, I would be dead.

[68]

"Now, which one of you people wants to start asking questions?" She gave an impromptu press conference that would have been the envy of the most consummate politician, and the afternoon news carried the story: Accused Murderer and Girlfriend Try to Slip Out of Tallahassee—Questioned at the Airport by Homicide Detective. Each of the media gave slightly different versions of the same story.

When I got back to Palmetto Bay I found four broken windows on the front of my house. Someone had painted the word "Commonist" on my garage door with black spray paint, but I knew what they meant. My phone was ringing, but when I picked up the receiver the caller hung up. This continued until I unplugged the telephone. I swept up the broken glass and four heavy beer bottles from my floor and cooked an early supper.

I parked my car inside the garage, the first time I'd ever done that, and woke twice during the night to the sounds of people running through my yard. After breakfast, I took my cup of coffee outside and hosed broken eggs from the walls. A television news truck was parked at the corner of the block, and as the camerman held a Minicam, the reporter pointed at me and said things I couldn't hear over the spray of the water. They packed up and zipped away without asking me anything, so I went back in the house and diagrammed the important steps in the case, trying to plot a course I could follow. A way out.

Mark came over a couple of days later and flopped down on the sofa, his face pasty, his confidence gone. "Jesus, Mac, I feel like I pulled out in front of a freight train," he said. "They've got me taking out the trash over there." He worked at the sleekest law firm a resort town could produce, and up until he filed against Birk, he'd been their golden boy.

"I've never seen this kind of pressure," he said. "I've never even heard of this kind of pressure." He stayed, and we talked about what had happened. He told me he thought he knew who told Birk where Katherine was the night she almost died. He promised me his name as soon as he was sure, not for some macho revenge but just so I'd know. I had to find out who was running things.

We talked about what we thought might happen next, and I told him I was considering giving Katherine a call to tell her it was time for her and Candy to drop out of sight. We hadn't been in touch since the airport, but she told me after the reporters left that Candy and James had been swamped by the press already. I was afraid they would let something slip about Limestone Creek. I pulled my ledger from the desk and wrote a check for Mark.

"Oh, boy!" he said, looking at it. "Now I can get those new shoes I've always wanted!"

"Kiss my ass," I said.

"Oh," Mark said, reaching into his briefcase with the check, "I got an express letter from Katherine this morning with some transcripts in it. That's why I came over." He pulled a small yellow envelope from the case. It had my first name written on it in green ink. "This was in the letter."

I took it from him but didn't open it. My fingers were gummy from the sizing I was using to caulk new pieces of glass into my windows. When Mark left I washed up and sat at my kitchen table. I opened the letter and spread the yellow pages out on my tabletop.

"This isn't a love letter," it said, "but I miss you. My bosses have been great at insulating me from the press and (did I tell you Candy's still living with Dr. Kuyatt and his family?) I'm living at the casino hotel now, so you can call me if you want to talk. I told James I wouldn't be coming back to him. I've been trying to do all the right things and please everyone for years, but I'm not sure if we're going to make it through this. I'm going to start pleasing myself.

"I never got the chance to ask about your black eye, but I hope it's better. Mac, no matter how this ends up, I'm glad we met.

"Call me,

"Kate."

I sat at the table a long time, looking out my window, then rereading the letter, I changed my dirty clothes and went for a drive. I don't know that I'd ever fit in here in Palmetto Bay, but I was definitely an outsider after my trip to Tallahassee. People cut in line ahead of me at the grocery store and dared me to complain. Gas station attendants shut off the fuel at the nozzle after I'd pumped a dollar or so. Cops cruised along behind me and waited for me to cross the center line. At least Birk didn't send anybody out to follow me around anymore. They were pretty sure I was no longer a bother, so I was able to visit my drops most nights without being seen.

There were various places around town where people I knew left messages for me in the old days, but none of the people I'd called had made an attempt to contact me. This night was no different, so I drove home, parked in the garage, and went inside. I reread Kate's letter, poured myself a small glass of wine, and walked into the bathroom. The house was dark and still, and I sat on the edge of my tub, holding the glass in both hands. I felt the peace that only Sheevers could provide, felt myself relax as we shared the silence, and knew my life was changing even as I clung to the past. I didn't want change, and I talked to Patty, alive in the darkness of my mind. Even though I knew this was the crap of which "Twilight Zone" was made, it was no less real, no less necessary than the air I breathed.

I talked about Katherine. I was afraid I would let her down, afraid I would fail. This case was overwhelming, and my cynicism, my indifference to life, wasn't insulating me the way it once did. I found myself wanting to live, and that felt like a betrayal of Sheevers and the life she gave for me. We sat together in the dark and listened to the little sounds of the world she'd loved so much. It was almost three o'clock, the bars were closed, and it was usually around this time that I lay in bed listening to the eggs splattering against the side of my house.

I heard a car ease to a stop out front and I slipped from the bathroom into the hall. I was embarrassed to be with Sheevers as they trashed our home. I stood still, waiting for the thump of the first egg, but it didn't come. Instead, I heard the tiny snapping sounds the screen-door spring makes when it's being stretched. It clicked quietly as someone opened the door slowly, cautiously. I walked into the bedroom and slipped my pistol from an open drawer, moved through the familiar house to the shadows behind my bookcase, out of the dim light from the aquarium.

The front door opened and a large man tiptoed into my living room, a paper bag in his hand. I stepped up behind him and stuck the cold muzzle of the gun into his neck. He made a little squeak. "Do exactly what I tell you to do," I said, "or I'll kill you." I put the fingers of my other hand on his back. "Get on your knees." He did. I walked to the sofa and sat on the arm, my pistol in line with his eyes. The bore of a nine-millimeter looks just a little bit larger than a train tunnel, especially when you're looking down it into infinity, and this guy's eyes were staring at the unfriendly face of God.

"Whatcha got there?" I asked, and he looked at the bag as though it were an alien thing before his eyes returned to the pistol. "Well?"

"Eggs," he said. He sounded very meek for a big man.

"Show me," I said. He reached into the bag, and it rustled as his hand dug frantically for an egg. He finally produced one and seemed almost proud that he'd done what I'd asked. He held it out to me.

"What were you going to do with those?" I asked, and he shrank back in fear. He didn't know there would be a test, and he had no answers ready. "Tell me." I made sure the pistol didn't waver. He said nothing.

"Maybe you were just hungry," I said, and he mumbled, 'Uh-huh."

[71]

He was beginning to think that he might get out of this alive, so I pushed the pistol into his forehead and said, "Eat the egg."

"What?" he said.

"Eat it, or I'll put a hole in you big enough to drop it through, do you understand?" He squeaked again and put the egg in his mouth. When he crunched down on it he made such a face that I almost turned away. His eyelids fluttered.

"How many more do you have in there?" I asked politely. He looked at the bag, and when he spoke his voice was round and hollow.

"Eleven," he said.

"Eat them all," I said. He started to protest, so I got to my feet and curled my finger around the trigger. His eyes crossed.

"Listen to me, you son of a bitch. You're a prowler in my home and I'll kill you in a heartbeat," I said. "And, except for having to clean your brains off my furniture, it won't bother me at all. Now eat those eggs."

His hand rustled into the bag for an egg, and he crunched into it, then made a gurgling sound. "If you throw up, you'll eat that too," I said. He sucked in a deep breath and swallowed another egg. Sweat poured down his face and I was getting sick watching him, so I moved around behind him and stuck the gun back into his neck. He repeated the process. Rustle, crunch, and gurgle. Rustle, crunch, gurgle.

I counted them down and told him to turn the bag over and shake it. My voice sounded a little rough and unsteady, but I don't think he noticed. He was whimpering as he shook the empty bag.

"Now get out of my house," I said. He took off like a runner out of the blocks and hit the screen door so hard it bounced off the outside wall and caught him on the shoulder as he plunged into the dark yard. I stood in the arch and watched as someone flung open the rear door of the car. He leapt inside.

A couple of excited voices asked questions as the car left the curb, then I heard a loud and obscene bubbling sound and the car swerved onto my neighbor's well-kept lawn. Loud curses came from the inside of the car as it bounced back onto the road, clipped a mailbox farther down the street, and barely made the turn at the corner. "My car, Goddamn it!" a male voice screeched in falsetto. "My car!"

I sat on the front step and let the pistol dangle between my knees. The bad thing was, these guys probably had nothing to do with Bob Birk. More than likely, they were just some concerned citizens, young guys listening to their parents and bosses gripe about people like me screwing up a good town; something that wouldn't have happened in "the old days." The good side was that nobody egged my house again.

TEN

When Mark Thornton filed the suit against Bob Birk, the press ignored it until Birk called a press conference on the marble steps of his office building. He stood between two giant American flags and spoke to a crowd of media that included a handful of national reporters and two network teams. He gave an eloquent speech using someone else's words. He said he'd been defamed by scum that had been paid off by the radical-liberal left. He said he welcomed the lawsuit that he would turn around and, with the help of "patriots and God," use it to show the corruption of ideals that threatened to destroy America.

I watched it on TV and waited for the days of egging and window-breaking to start up again, but it didn't happen. Going to town was still no fun, and I had yet to hear from a single contact. I knew Mel Shiver would be very careful, but I still expected to have had some word from him. I was feeling pretty lonesome, and I drove around town, found a comfortable pay phone, and called Katherine. We talked for a long time about nothing and I hung up, believing there was a solution to this case. There had to be.

On the way home around midnight I drove to the marina and stopped my car. I sidled to the railing, and after glancing around, I got on my hands and knees. I poked my head through the railing and reached into a piece of broken concrete on the underside of the seawall, expecting nothing but finding a thin envelope. It had been doubled over and wedged into the crack, and there was only one person who would have done it. The last on my list of people I thought would still be there, willing to help. A man with a lot to lose.

I tucked the envelope into my shirt and stood, leaning on the rail for at least twenty minutes before I returned to my car and went home.

I sat in my comfortable chair and turned on the lamp. Willis Traxler's letters were always a challenge to read, not because he was stupid but because he was illiterate. Raised on the edge of Palmetto

Bay in one of the isolated pulpwood communities, Willis had had his priorities in line early, tattooed there by the rise and fall of the river and its impact on his family. Everybody worked six days a week. The men spent their days in the woods from "can to can't," as they say, filling dilapidated trucks with pulpwood and huge, grotesquely formed roots of southern pine called fat-lightered, because they are heavy, and thick with turpentine. Just one sliver can kindle a fire. The women raised the children until they could work alongside the adults, and cleaned the houses of wealthy people in Palmetto Bay. On Sundays they would go to church, then come home and work on the trucks and chain saws until bedtime.

Like many small southern towns, Palmetto Bay hired its locals for the low-end jobs and brought in management from the North and the Midwest. Faulkner's Snopes family, great as they were for literature, left a taint on the good people who quit school to work and always smelled of diesel fuel and turpentine. Willis said "laigs" instead of legs, "aigs" instead of eggs, and was called a redneck by the people he worked for. He was a nonentity, and the more compassionate cluck-clucked about the victims of this "archaic system." My favorite quote came from a well-dressed, middle-aged couple from Chicago who confided in me that "We didn't know how bad the education system was down here until we come down and seen it."

Willis was so glad to have a real job that he ignored the daily insults, and even though promotions were seldom seen, he now had almost eighteen years in as a sheriff's deputy. He took me under his wing a long time ago and taught me how to fish for largemouth bass, how to entice a giant from the black water with an artificial lure and make him rip open the surface and dance. There are some people in the world who simply like each other from the start, and we were like that. I didn't see much of him anymore, but we were still friends.

"To Mack," the note, paper-clipped to three folded sheets of white paper, said, "I herd them say the girl was rapped on june 12"—that was the date given by Mark in the lawsuit—'I fond these and I copied them. Maby you will use them. Willis.' "

I pulled the sheets from the note and unfolded them. One was a photocopy of an old Sheriff's Department log, authorizing five drivers and cars to escort local dignitaries to Omni property for something special at the Limestone Creek Men's Club. The date of the event was June the twelfth, five years back. The second sheet was another old log entry sending eight deputies to the Sunset Hotel for security later that same night.

The third sheet was a bad copy of a hospital report. It showed emergency-room treatment of two teenage girls for multiple bruises. One girl had a broken wrist. The date on the report was June the twelfth. The report had been rubber-stamped "Paid."

Willis didn't just find these reports. He had to have searched for them in the files, hours or perhaps days of looking over his shoulder as he dug through the records warehouse. Three potentially powerful pieces of information after weeks of nothing. I owed him a big favor.

I was excited again, and I began to pace the house. My mind turned cartwheels trying to assimilate this new information, and I wanted more. What happened at the Men's Club that could turn community leaders into cowboys at the end of a cattle drive? The enigmatic pairing of the first two bits of information with the hospital report created large playgrounds for my imagination and became puzzles to be solved.

The next two days went by unnoticed as I pulled the bag of facts from the garbage and laid them out again with my three new pieces. I tried to find out if the girls who'd been treated at the hospital that night were still in the area. I called people with the same last names but got nowhere. It was possible Candace had been close to them sometime that evening, and, under the circumstances, they might remember her.

I was sitting on the floor eating boiled peanuts and shuffling the facts around when Mark called. Before I could say hello he shouted, "Channel Five, now!" and hung up. I brushed a mound of peanut shells off my lap and crawled to the TV, turned it on, and changed the channel. There, in a fan of microphones, was a pretty young woman with dark-blond hair and no makeup. Her eyes were large, and they darted back and forth as people shouted questions at her. I knew how that felt.

"No, no," she said. "There were a lot of reasons not to talk about it. There still are." Another woman stepped up beside her and looked just about as nervous. A local lawyer named Bobby Stearns stood behind them. The second woman took her turn.

"We've lived with this a long time," she said. Her hair was jet black and it made her pale skin look like milk. A microphone whistled. "And there are other women out there who've been afraid this day would come." She looked over at the other woman. "But, to tell the truth, I'm glad it's here. I worked for Tommy Lovett for over a year, and my parents never knew about the Sunset Hotel." She dropped her eyes to the podium, and I dropped my heart into my stomach.

I don't remember taking a breath for at least five minutes. It took that long for the woman to tell of the abuse and debauchery of Lovett and company, the pay-for-sex business with young girls from his pool hall, and, like music to my ears, the revelation of Bob Birk as a regular customer.

The special report switched back to the newsroom, where anchorman Todd Franklin, tie loose and white sleeves rolled up to show the timeliness of the event, looked at a small monitor.

"Glen?" A crackling pause before the on-scene reporter answered. "Glen, what have you heard form the Birk headquarters?"

"Well, Todd," said a young bearded reporter brought into split screen, "Bill Norris, Mr. Birk's campaign manager, told me just now that his people are trying to find out what's behind this . . . well, he called it the latest smear campaign. He said they'd be issuing a statement by news time this afternoon."

I sat in front of the television and watched two game shows, ate an entire bag of peanuts, and waited for the local news. The lead story was about Wanda Dinkins and Linda White and their confessions of sex and perversion at the Sunset Hotel, but this time their lawyer did most of the talking, and his words, though sensational, were carefully chosen.

I was breathless. The case of Candace Furay versus the world was taking on a new life, one that reminded me that Candy was only one of the victims and that others had suffered too. I wondered if more would come forward, and, though Birk's damage-control team was incredible, they managed only to douse the flames. It didn't take much effort to see where it still smoldered.

His people painted Birk as the only victim, a man at the mercy of a vengeful left-wing liberal attempt to bring down the one man with the vision and power to stop the downfall of America. They colored the women's reputations, implied collusion with a conspiracy to ruin Bob Birk. They suggested a payoff had been made and that the people of the Panhandle wouldn't put up with it.

By the time the ten-o'clock news came on, two more women had come forward with horror stories of Tommy Lovett and the Sunset Hotel. One said she'd been with Bob Birk several times and she remembered the night Candy Furay was raped. Mark Thornton came over with pizza and beer, and later we drove to a pay phone and called Katherine. She wanted to collect Candace and fly down to join the ranks, but Mark cautioned her to stay where she was. He told me later he suspected his bosses, Barrett, Barrett and Finch, of informing Birk about Katherine's visit to Tallahassee.

The next day three women came separately to the press to support the others, and Palmetto Bay divided itself into two camps. One side held a religious rally and all-night gospel sing, handing out glossy bumper stickers that announced, "Bob Birk's Enemies are America's Enemies." A front-page photo in the Friday paper showed a room full of Birk supporters wearing the stickers across their T-shirted chests. Friday afternoon I found out just how good Birk's team was.

Just before news time, one of the women who had come alone to the press the day before shouted tearfully to a news team that, yes, she had been paid by some lawyers from south Florida to say what she had said—all of it lies—and, yes, she was sure the other women had too. She said the lawyers told her that if Bob Birk dropped out of the race for governor, she would get a thousand-dollar bonus.

Community reaction was instant outrage, and the denials of the other women went unheard in the uproar. The woman who had confessed to taking the money to ruin Birk quickly disappeared, and the once-bitten press made no attempt to find her. Patriotic rallies were held Saturday, not only in the Panhandle but all the way to the Florida Keys. Birk showed up at a massive rally held by the Cuban community of Miami. Red, white, and blue banners lined the route of his motorcade, and "NBC Nightly News" ran a feature on his campaign.

The other six women held their ground with their lawyers and a terrified Mark Thornton. Two of them were beaten by a group of angry women in the courthouse parking lot after their meeting with the grand jury.

On the live Sunday-morning broadcast from the First Baptist Church of Palmetto Bay, Bob Birk received a standing ovation from the congregation as the youth choir sang "God Bless America." I drove to the convenience store and called Katherine, then held the phone for a long time as she cried.

I really wanted to ask her to call the whole thing off, to keep Candy in therapy until she could accept the deaths of her friends and to forget this goddamned town. I leaned on the blue bubble that housed the pay phone and looked at the pompous headline on Sunday's paper, boasting Birk's virtue in patriotically colored inks. I watched Bob Birk bumper stickers go by on everything from police cars to skateboards. I felt hopeless and lost.

We said good-bye and I hung up. A horn blew, and I watched a man flip me the finger as he drove past. The cashier ignored me for a long time but finally took my money, and I walked out with milk and a

[77]

package of bear claws. I had hoped to soften up Bob Birk, to weaken him with the rape charge. He should have been on the defensive, punch drunk and prone to mistakes, but, instead, he was stronger.

On Wednesday morning the grand jury allowed Reverend Bo Treadwell of the First Baptist Church to speak to them behind closed doors, and just after noon the same day, they threw out Candace Furay's case against Bob Birk. The foreman of the grand jury said there wasn't enough evidence to warrant a trial.

Reverend Treadwell explained to the press that he felt it necessary to let the grand jury know that Mr. Birk was a good, Christian man with decent values and that his contributions to the community and to the church should be considered.

I felt something begin to uncoil in the darkest part of my soul, something I hadn't known for five years. It slipped into the warmth of my blood and wound around my heart. I saw the frightened and bitter faces of the women betrayed by justice, and I could see them as they were before, that day so long ago when I interviewed them with their parents. Frightened children who had trembled in the presence of their angry fathers and bewildered mothers as I looked down on them from my lofty perch. I thought of the years this shame lay uneasy, touching their lives in everything they'd done, and I knew what it had taken for them to come forward, what it cost them in the eyes of their town.

I remembered their young faces that day five years before when I took their statements, and I realized, too late, how arrogant I'd been, how little consideration I had given their pain. Suddenly, time turned upside down and I was standing inside the front door of my house again, excited by the fact that we had finally wrapped up the case and were on our way to success. I was in my best suit and tie, and I loosened the knot, unbuttoned the collar button, and called out to Sheevers. She didn't answer, and I walked past an aquarium filled with brightly colored fish to the kitchen, then into the hall, where I opened the door and found her mutilated body in such an ordinary room.

I'm not a complicated man. I never lay in Sheevers's arms and wondered what I was missing, what another woman might do for me. I was booked solid through eternity, and we spent our nights planning a future that would never happen. Since her death I had dodged any responsibility for tomorrow and turned a blind eye to the problems of the world. Watching Brother Bo, as he was affectionately called, charm the TV screen that Wednesday afternoon did something of biblical proportions to me. His voice was Joshua's trumpet at Jericho, and my walls came tumblin' down.

I have a friend who believes that space is cluttered with inert comets, great balls of ice that not only replenish the earth's water supply but are filled with mischief. He says some are full of viruses and nasty gases that push the world to the brink of madness and death, and some are pocketed with spores of knowledge and evolutionary transistors that suck us in one side and shoot us out the other in a snakes-and-ladders game of survival of the fittest. He told me the mysterious sonic booms heard here and there around the world are just the sounds of us colliding with another ball of ice—maybe good, maybe bad. A game of chance.

When I came out of my fog that Wednesday afternoon with the drone of Channel Five's weatherman in the background, I thought I heard a sonic boom. I drove to a phone booth and called Katherine at work, left a message, and waited there for her to call me back. When she did, she sounded distant and detached.

"Mac," she said, "I've been thinking about it, and I believe it's time to stop. Candace is a basket case and my life's in pieces right now. Somewhere in my mind I convinced myself I could save Candy." She hesitated. "Save you, too, I guess. Save the world—" She choked on the words.

"Fuck," she said. She sniffed and cleared her throat. "Let's forget it, Mac. It's not worth it."

"It's strange, Katherine," I said. "I was going to say the same thing to you yesterday. But, now that I've thought it over, there's no way I'm going to quit. If I don't stop these bastards the world won't be worth living in and, all of a sudden, I want to live a little longer.

"I think you have saved me," I said. "I think I've finally figured out why living is better than dying, and I don't want to forget it. You just hold on, keep it together out there, and I'll see if I can't make a little noise."

"Oh, Mac." Her voice changed with each word. "Do you really mean it? Do you think there's still a chance?"

"Hell, yes," I said. "There's still a chance." I didn't know what I was talking about, but I was tired of seeing them win all the time and I was sick of seeing Katherine's hopes crushed every time she turned around. Even if it was a lie, it was something to believe in, a reason to hope. And sometimes that's all that makes the difference between living and dying. "I'm tired of these jerks pushing me around." I could hear people talking around her. "I have to go now, Katherine, but I'll be in touch."

[79]

"Hey?" she said, and I waited. "Please don't get hurt, Mac, I want to see you again."

"Well, okay," I said. "But it's not fair. You get to get hurt."

"It's not all it's cracked up to be."

"Speaking of cracked up, how's the jaw?"

"I'm okay," she said. "I'll be fine as long as I know you're safe. I'm worried about Candy, though. She's really under a lot of stress, and Dr. Kuyatt is getting pushy about telling the world about Omni."

Just the thought of that gave me the willies. "Tell him to wait until I call back. I don't care what he wants to do, he can't let this out until I get some things done here. Tell him to give me two weeks. It's not that long."

"Okay."

"I'll be in touch," I said. "Take care."

I drove home and checked the mail. In the small stack of bills and junk was a letter that, even without a return address, I knew was from Mel. I turned it over and checked the seal, then looked in the corners for slits, but it seemed okay. Before I went inside I walked across my yard and checked out my home. I had spent a lot of time over the last few years working around the house, and it seemed to be holding up through my recent neglect, although the grass needed mowing. Mockingbirds sang to me from the electric wires as I climbed the ladder and checked my roof. Satisfied, I went inside and opened the letter from Mel. It was brief and urgent.

"I need some evidence that the Contras were at Omni," the letter said. "And I need it soon. Without it, I can't get the right people to listen. This thing is bigger than we believed, friend." It was signed, "Mel."

I reread the letter before I threw it away, then opened the others, sat at my desk, and paid the bills. I thought of calling Mark to work up a will leaving everything to Katherine, but it not only seemed melodramatic, I could think of no reason why she would want it, or the hassle of disposing of it. She had her own job, her own stuff.

I pulled out all the clippings I had collected on Omni, Inc., and after dinner I sat down and studied them. There were brochures on the luxury homes that circled Omni's twin lakes and met at a huge clubhouse that sat between them, offering me the rare opportunity to not only own one but, by doing so, become a part of the "Dynamic New Future of Northwest Florida." I had copies of topo maps and aerial photographs from both the courthouse and a realtor who, for some reason, thought I represented a group of Germans interested in buying a large tract of land alongside Omni.

I had spent a couple of mornings at Limestone Creek during my "egg days," walking the trails and taking pictures. I even proved to myself that I could still climb a tree, and as I sat at my table with a magnifying glass looking over the blowups, I saw an imposing structure I knew to be the Men's Club. I could see enough details to guess where it was in relation to the surrounding buildings, and with the help of aerial photos, I planned my entry and exit.

I noticed on the brochures that moonlight rides on horseback and several nature trails were underlined as positive parts of the Omni Lifestyle, and I hoped that meant a minimum of electronic security, but I had no way of knowing for sure. I couldn't think of a way to find out more, and, besides, I was tired of waiting. Maybe a bit of the "blaze of glory" mentality still hung on, but I wanted this thing settled.

Bob Birk had a big lead for his party's nomination over the incumbent governor, and his two opposition candidates were losing ground. The primaries were just around the corner, and I was afraid that once he cleared that hurdle he'd be unstoppable.

I studied the maps of Limestone Creek that I'd picked up at the canoe livery and tried to memorize them. When I called Thursday morning to book a buyer's tour of the Omni grounds I was told the resort was closed until Tuesday. I got indignant and said my business had me in another part of the world by then and I would think they could make an exception. They surprised me by saying "Sorry." Better luck next time. Whatever the reason, it was important enough for salespeople to give up their enormous commissions. I studied the newspapers for a clue and finally found a tiny article that mentioned a formal get-together at Omni on Friday night. It wasn't a come-on to draw a crowd but only stated its existence. One of those either-you're-invited-or-you're-not things, and I immediately wanted to stick my nose in and see what was going on. There were a couple of problems: I wasn't invited. They didn't like me.

I called the Men's Club, told them I was a caterer, and asked for the assistant manager's name. Then I called the caterers and told them I was the assistant manager of the Men's Club. I said I wanted to know if they were going to have any trouble delivering all they'd agreed on. Two of them said they didn't know what I was talking about, one guy tried to give me a better deal, and the fourth person said everything was ready and they'd be there at six o'clock to begin setting up before the band showed up. I told her I could send a man over to help but she said, "No, thank you." It was worth a try.

There were only three bands in the area that could play the kind of music they'd want to hear out there, and I found the right one on the second call. Larry Lemon and the Lancers were ready, Larry told me, and they'd be there at eight o'clock, as agreed. They would play from nine until one, with a fifteen-minute break every hour.

"Do you know 'The Hokey-Pokey'?" I said. There was a hesitation. "Yes, sir."

"It's Mr. Birk's favorite song," I said, then hung up.

I drove to town and cruised the pawnshops until I found a trumpet and case. I went to Sears and brought beige pants and a bright red blazer and hoped the Lancers hadn't changed their image, though there wasn't much chance of that. I found a large black jumpsuit and decided to buy it too.

My plan looked good every other hour as Friday approached. On alternate hours I knew I was an idiot and that I would be dead before I ever heard "The Hokey-Pokey." It seemed as though it might work. Nobody paid attention to musicians, or expected anything out of them.

I left the house in jeans and a dark-green T-shirt and drove away unnoticed. Clouds obscured the half-moon as I eased my car to a stop on a dirt road north of the county bridge that crossed Limestone Creek just east of Omni's main gate. It was the place I'd reconnoitered, the spot where Candy Furay had watched her friends die as she sat quietly in the dark.

I opened the trunk and pulled out a small inflatable boat and pumped it up. I stripped off my clothes and put on the Sears outfit, then pulled the jumpsuit on over it. The trumpet case fit into the bow and left enough room for me to huddle over the frail plastic oars. There were so many things wrong with this plan, so many things that could go wrong, that I wasted no more time thinking about them.

The current was swift and branches hung down everywhere, spinning the little boat around like a top. I held on and forgot about the oars until I was under the bridge, then used them to brake myself and finally slip out of the flow into a still pool. I stepped out gingerly, grimacing as my bare feet touched the icy water. The horn case made an adequate seat, and I put on my shoes before slipping the boat up onto the bank. I looked through the ragged, rusted sheets of corrugated tin, the last remnant of the old fence that skirted the creek, and saw a wide field of low grass and small pines, black as ink and crowned, far away, by the floodlighted splendor of the Limestone Creek Men's Club.

I pulled a piece of tin aside and slid through carefully, then reached back and brought the trumpet case to me. I swallowed. Sometimes you reach a point where you can only act. There are no more words, no more plans—you have no room for doubts. Headlights of cars sparkled in the night as the limousines circled in front of the club and spewed wealthy white people into their invitation-only corral. It was too far away to see if there were many guards outside, and I moved silently, listening for any sounds of men or dogs. I turned back and looked at the fence, got my bearings, then turned again and worked my way across the dark field.

ELEVEN

When I got within rock-throwing distance of the parking lot I circled around to the back of the building and stood behind the catering van, stripped off the jumpsuit, and took the trumpet from the case. I checked my watch and leaned against the truck to wait. The band took their first break and I stepped into the parking lot, trumpet dangling from one hand as I wiped my brow with a handkerchief I held in the other.

I took on a casual gait and glanced around, but could see no one moving. I wandered along the back and checked doors until I found one unlocked. It opened without an alarm going off and I stepped inside a long white hallway. There were three solid doors set into the left wall and one in the center of the right. I could hear the muffled sounds of a party from somewhere above. I wandered to the door on my right and leaned forward, listening. The knob turned in my hand, but before I could open it, I heard the unmistakable sound of an M-16's bolt being set. Lock and load. I stretched a goofy grin across my face and turned around. A uniformed soldier wearing no insignia stood in the middle doorway with the muzzle pointed at my chest.

"Jesus Christ!" I said. "You scared the shit out of me!" I wiped my face with the handkerchief. "In fact, I don't think I need to find a bathroom now, thanks to you."

"There are no bathrooms in here, sir," the young soldier said.

"Well, there has to be one somewhere in this fucking Taj Mahal," I said, twisting my trumpet hand over to glance at my watch. "Goddamn! Five minutes left to take a leak and I still have to find my way back to the bandstand." I laughed and shook my head. "The last door I tried, I wound up in the parking lot.

"Can you at least tell me where the hell I am?" I asked. "And please stop pointing that gun at me!" The soldier kept the rifle right

[84]

where it was and nodded his head toward the exit door. I took a quick peek at the door I almost opened.

"You'll have to leave now, sir," he said. "Good luck."

"Luck?" I said. "Have you been listening to the crap we're playing? I don't need luck, I need a lobotomy."

The soldier laughed. I opened the door to the parking lot and walked out singing, "Feelings/nothing more than feelings." The outer, nonconditioned air was sticky and warm. "I hope you don't kill me/ then I'll have no feelings . . ." I heard him laugh again as the door closed behind me. I was stunned. There, inside a private men's club on private land, was a uniformed soldier armed with a loaded M-16 and fully prepared to kill. I had to go back in. The music started up again, and I could hear bass notes and laughter through the walls.

I turned the knob slowly and pulled the door open. There would be no excuses if he discovered me this time. I hugged the left wall and worked my way down until I was directly across from the other door. I listened but could hear nothing, so I took a deep breath, quickly crossed the hall, and stepped through the door, closing it behind me.

The caterers didn't even look up when I came in, but kept piling food on a long table covered with a dark-green cloth that hung to the gray-tiled floor. "Put those down first!" a woman shouted angrily. "No! Those!" I ducked behind a handcart stacked high with folding chairs just as the door opened and the same soldier stuck his head in, looked around slowly, and disappeared back into the hall.

The caterers waddled away and I crawled from behind the handcart to look around. It was a large room, smooth and businesslike with several rows of folding chairs already set up and facing a modern, lighted podium. A giant-screen TV hung from a low ceiling behind the podium, and a ball of speakers protruded from the wall under it. A video camera sat on its tripod and stared at an empty stage. I heard people talking and I ducked down again. "Wait!" a man said. "We'll need those chairs."

I felt like all three stooges as I crawled under the table, trying not to drag the trumpet, getting the heel of my shoe caught in the green tablecloth. I heard the click of shoes just inches from my fingers and then the sound of the handcart squeaking away across the floor. People began filing into the room, and I smelled cigar smoke.

For twenty minutes I lay perfectly still on the hard tile, propped up on my elbow, watching shiny leather tips of shoes slip back and forth under the tablecloth like busy mice as the men above munched on the catered treats. The top of my head scraped against the rough underside of the table. I thought to myself, *I'm a grown man, reasonably intelligent, semieducated, and I'm hiding under a table in a room filled with men, some probably my age.*

A public-address system was switched on and little electronic pops and squeals bounced around the room. A man's voice, amplified but off mike, said, "Check the video camera, Stanley, then set these levels." The men at the table stopped talking.

"Gentlemen." The speaker's voice was strong and self-confident. "Please be seated. I have much to discuss with you while our friends and families enjoy the party upstairs, so please hold all questions until I've finished." Footsteps shuffled away from me and I could hear the squeak of folding chairs being dragged over the floor. The room lights dimmed, so I lay down and peeked out from under the tablecloth. A soft spotlight washed the speaker in a bluish-white glow. He was an older man, in his mid-sixties. He had close-cropped white hair and a little white mustache.

"First, let me tell each and every one of you that your actions have not gone unnoticed. You men have invested in the future of this country in the last few years, and it is my opinion that, soon, yours will be the patriotism that all others will be judged by.

"It is a new world, and there will be a new order. This new world is exciting, but dangerous; a world in which there will be no room for amateurs in government." He scanned each face. "America has survived all these years because of something more than a population willing to fight for it. It's sad to say, gentlemen, but we owe our survival to dumb luck as much as to anything else." The room was so quiet, I wondered if any of these men dared to breathe. A tall, slender man I guessed was Stanley stood bent over the video camera, watching the man through a tiny window.

As this speaker continued his powerful speech, I felt a chill that didn't come from lying on the cold tile floor. He talked about the Middle East and the changing face of Europe and Asia and said we could no longer afford the luxury of a haphazard government that couldn't make decisions. "Look at the Congress," he said. "What do you think of Congress?" There was a chorus of boos and catcalls.

"Exactly!" he shouted. "They have outlived their usefulness in the job of keeping America secure. They are simply bottomless pits of ego and, if left to them, our standing in the world will be gone. And we can't have that." The room stayed silent, with an undercurrent of murmured conversations. "The time has come when it isn't enough to have opinions. Men are going to have to have convictions! To take a stand for their beliefs. And I don't mean over dinner with the wife, I mean in public. At their places of business and in government."

He said people no longer knew what they wanted and were prone to follow any scheme, any diversion. He told these men it was their job to decide a direction and to make sure it followed a well-defined plan. "We have set our goal on the year 2000." He took the microphone in his hand and drifted away from the podium, his forehead wrinkled in thought. "Not far away now, friends. The year 2000 will bring forth a new America, a single-minded America that will lead the rest of the world into the new order. We will be the leader, not one of the followers." And then he gave them the plan.

Even Mel, in his deepest paranoid fantasies, would have come unglued. I thought of his letter and wondered if he'd found traces of this plan. The nation's drug czar had been on a speaking tour that contained a teaser about orphanages that would be created to separate children from drug-infested communities and families and give them a chance to live drug-free. Inner cities would be reshaped to offer "economic opportunities." Then the speaker dropped the bombshell.

"As you well know, military bases are, and always have been, the backbone of your economy. Well, gentlemen, by the year 2000, giant military bases will be a thing of the past. Kiss 'em good-bye." The collective intake of breath in that room drained the oxygen supply and left everyone dizzy. He let them think about it for over a minute.

"This is not the end," he said. "It is the beginning. The beginning of a new America, an unconfused America, and men like Mr. Bob Birk will be at the helm." A thundering applause shook the room. "My friends, we have set in motion a restructuring of government in Florida that will make it a model for the rest of the nation, for the rest of the world. And you men will play leadership roles in it.

"For you see, gentlemen, leadership is the single most important product we supply to the world. Let them have their factories and their spiraling inflation. We will trim down and rebuild a nation that will be the envy of them all, and the wheels have already been set in motion." It wasn't a long speech, but I thought it would never end. Military bases would be converted to drug detention centers and state-controlled "orphanages" where disadvantaged children would be taught trades, honing them in ultramodern shops that would provide cheap, dependable, nonunion merchandise for the state. Everything from envelopes to computers would be made in these state centers. This would also relieve the overburdened public school system so that

[87]

Florida's other children, the leaders of tomorrow, could begin to learn again, could prepare for their futures.

The speaker told us that the Contras were conceived in Washington, D.C., and designed to be the prototype of the future "supercadre" of special-forces troops that would be housed around the state on private land in privately financed minibases close to urban centers. Funded by industry and private donations, these troops could be mobilized at a moment's notice to isolate the drug community from the rest of the population if the need arose. Changes in drug laws would legalize the sale of drugs in these controlled areas and the sales would be heavily taxed.

"If you think Prohibition was a failure," the speaker said, "then you simply aren't seeing history for what it is. Prohibition was only a tool, just the time it took for the government to establish an orderly line of supply to meet the demand. To cut out the wildcatters and those who wouldn't play by the rules. It was never the object of the government to remove liquor forever from the American people." He drank from a tall glass.

"Drugs aren't going to go away," he said. "That's reality. But the killing and the destruction of law and order don't have to be the reality of the drug trade. The overlapping of drug problems on the lives of decent people need not be tolerated. We feel we can set up supply lines and bonded agents to handle these lower forms who will always use drugs, and tax them to provide services to the good people of the state of Florida.

"Each of you will receive a copy of our detailed plans charting the future of your state, and a short letter telling you what will be expected of you. There will be substantial rewards offered you as members of this leadership team. You have never had in your possession documents so vital and so sensitive, and they are not to be taken home and shared with the wife," he said. "Or your mistress." There were chuckles in the room.

"There is a good reason no women are in this room," he said. "Women are not leaders. They do not have the capacity to lead." He held up his hands and smiled. "Please don't misunderstand me, gentlemen. I have a wonderful wife and we've been together for over thirty years. When it comes to nurturing, to support and love, there's no one I like better. But I don't tell her what I do day by day, and I never will.

"Things have gotten mixed up in the world, and that's what's gone wrong. We've allowed malcontents the right to make decisions that affect the rest of us. You are on the front line of a new America that

[88]

will take control again." He went on with his pep talk to this small group of power brokers, and I wondered how many other groups he'd stroked this way. I also began to wonder how I was going to get out of there alive. I felt like the guy in *Invasion of the Body Snatchers* just before he ran screaming onto the highway.

I looked at the speaker, at Bob Birk, and at a few others sitting behind him. These weren't the smooth officials sent to pacify the public, these were the rough-and-tumble boys, the left hand of government that picks your pocket as the right hand waves the flag.

When he wrapped up his speech he held up a videocassette tape and said, "I have a surprise for you all after dinner. We have a copy of the event that started it all several years ago, right here at Omni." A splatter of applause like frying bacon died down when he placed the tape on the podium.

"The colonel's speech is still an inspiration, and we thought, since several of you missed it, tonight would be a good time to relive the event." He nodded to someone who turned up the lights, and I dropped the cloth to the floor.

"Mr. Birk assures me we have the finest seafood dinners you have ever tasted just across the hall." The speaker moved away from the microphone. "So, if you will join us?" Chair legs scooted on the floor and I heard the crowd shuffle out of the room.

"Stanley," the speaker's voice was fatherly, "after you rewind that one and set up the colonel's tape for viewing, you may join us for dinner."

"Thank you, sir!" an eager voice replied. The door opened and closed and I lifted the cloth slowly. Stanley was still bent over the video camera as I slipped out from under the table, and I almost died of fright when my ankles popped, louder than firecrackers. Luckily, the man was lost in another world as he tinkered with the machine. I glanced at the door as I crept up behind him.

It wouldn't have been good enough to get me into professional football, but the dropkick I delivered to Stanley's nuts from behind lifted him up on his tippy-toes and his hands shot straight up over his head as if he was giving me credit for a field goal. When he came down he bent double like an inchworm, and I had to crouch down to punch him. His long head snapped sideways on his long neck, and when he hit the floor Stanley curled up in a ball.

The tape in the camera was still rewinding, and I punched every button on the machine twice before it stopped and ejected. Stanley moaned. I grabbed the tape and the cassette from the podium and stuck one in each pocket of the blazer as I hurried to the table. I picked up the trumpet and opened the door. There, alone in the hall, was the same young soldier I'd met earlier. Upstairs, the band was playing "The Hokey-Pokey."

"You?" he said as I brought the trumpet up and connected solidly with his chin. His eyelids drooped, but to my surprise, he didn't fall. His hands fumbled for the M-16 and I slammed the bent bell down over his flat-topped cap. He dropped to his knees, and I slipped the rifle from his arm as he fell forward onto the tiles. The two smacks with the trumpet bent it out of shape and sounded louder than a courthouse clock, but I had already grabbed the jumpsuit and was halfway to the fence when the yelling started. Men shouted in anger and confusion, and to my horror I heard the rotors of a helicopter begin whumping through a high-pitched whine.

The space between me and the fence seemed roughly the size of Nebraska and the cassettes were lead weights in my pockets. I ran over the little trees and bounced off the big ones. My blazer caught on a jagged edge of tin and ripped as I dove through the fence. I threw down the balled-up jumpsuit, shrugged out of the blazer, and looked back to see a helicopter's running lights lifting into the sky over the Men's Club. I removed the tapes and spread the red jacket over the floor of the yellow boat, then pushed it back into the current with my foot. I grabbed the jumpsuit, slipped it on, and started running north along the creek bank. Men were shouting commands just a few hundred yards away, and even though I carried a loaded M-16 in my right hand I doubted I would use the rifle under any circumstances. It wasn't as though these men were real soldiers. They were renegades, as far as I was concerned, but I didn't want to get into a firefight with them when I had only one clip. I much preferred the run-and-hide method.

The chopper, a Blackhawk, swung over the bridge, and I waited until it nosed southward before I stepped out from under the abutment. As I climbed over the limestone banks in the dark I pushed the cassettes into my pockets, and when I heard machine-gun fire, I stopped in my tracks and looked up at the Blackhawk as it negotiated over the heavily forested creek, its searchlights flashing through the branches like strobes, like the slow flares that used to illuminate the magnificent landscape of Vietnam.

The chopper pilot held the tail in the air as it skittered sideways above the creek, and the gunner cleared a right-of-way with his heavy firepower. Tracers whizzed through the trees, and somewhere below, the little yellow boat was taking a beating. Small fires began dancing on the banks. I turned my back on the scene and made my way slowly upstream to my car.

I drove with the lights off until I came to the paved county road, then headed carefully to my house. I didn't think they'd get around to suspecting me until much later, and though this hadn't gone as well as I'd hoped in one way, it certainly turned out to be a bonanza in another. I had the evidence Mel wanted, and all I had to do was stay alive long enough to get it to him. I decided it was time to pack a bag and disappear from Palmetto Bay until I could get the tapes safely to Mel. My first move would be to call Katherine and let her know the time had come, but as I opened my front door and turned on the lights, my telephone rang.

"Hello?" I tried to sound calm, but Katherine's hysterical shouting on the other end unnerved me. "Wait a minute!" I shouted back at her. "Katherine, what is it? What's wrong?"

"They're dead!" she screamed at me. "They're all dead, Mac!" Suddenly, the ground was falling out from under me.

"Who, Katherine? Who's dead?" I fumbled for control.

"Oh, God." She broke down then. "Mac, they killed everyone." She was gulping for air.

"Please, Katherine," I begged her. "Slow down and tell me. Catch your breath and I'll hold on." I forgot about a suitcase and grabbed a couple of hampers of clean clothes, and with the receiver pinched between my chin and shoulder, I moved them to the front door. I could hear a woman crying in the background, and I tried to picture where Katherine could be.

"Hey, we can't let it fall apart now," I said. "I need you. I want you to get Candace and get out of town tonight."

"Mac," she interrupted, "Candy called me this morning and told me that Dr. Kuyatt had gone to see Senator Teall. She begged him not to go, to wait until you called, but he wouldn't listen." Katherine said something away from the mouthpiece and the other woman stopped crying. "She was scared, so I drove over and picked her up at the doctor's house. He told Senator Teall everything, Mac, and they just showed it on the news." She worked fiercely on her breathing.

"They talked about the Contras and the murders?" I asked.

"No." She sighed. "Dr. Kuyatt's office burned to the ground this afternoon. When the police went to his house to tell him, they found him and his family dead. Someone shot them all, even their two children." I became aware of all the miles between us. "They won't stop until they find us, Mac. And now they know all about you too."

[91]

"Damn," I said, waiting as she tried to soothe the other woman. Valuable seconds passed before she came back to the phone. "Is Candy with you?"

"Yes."

"Listen to me. I don't care how you do it, but get out of Las Vegas right now. Go to the place where you met Sack-o and Van Zeti and I'll be there." I heard a car pass the house and I looked out the window into the night.

"Do it now, Katherine," I said. "I have the evidence we need to hang these people, and we can win! But it won't mean anything to me if you're not safe. I couldn't take it if you got hurt, do you understand?"

"I think I do, Mac," she said, her voice almost normal. "I feel the same about you." There was a pause. "I'll be . . . we'll be okay."

"Just get there, pal," I said. "I'll make sure they're expecting you. Do you think you can find it?"

"Oh, yes," she said. "No problem."

"Believe in me, Katherine," I said, and hung up. I tossed the M-16 on top of my stacks of clothes before I ran into the bathroom. I grabbed a handful of supplies and stuffed them into a shaving bag, then went quickly into the bedroom to grab the cash I'd withdrawn from the bank. I slipped the pistol into my belt, scooped up a box of ammunition, and took it all into the living room. I pushed everything between two piles of clean shirts, turned off the lights, and took one last look at my home.

What I had was an absurd stack of supplies, but I knew they would be quick when the news from Nevada reached them. This vigilante government and its army had worked as fast as fire ants when I stirred them up at the Men's Club. I was still amazed at how they had reacted instantly to my intrusion. They were inexperienced, but good. And they wouldn't be inexperienced long.

I kicked the screen door open and stepped out into the night, scanning the yard over the top of my tall stack of belongings. My foot missed the last step and I lost my balance, went airborne, and fell on my stomach beside the jasmine, my clothes fanning out on the grass in front of me. My angry words to myself died in my throat when I looked toward my clothes and saw a man standing on the dark driveway.

"Clay," he said. "You must be the original hard-luck ace." He knelt down and started throwing clothes back into the baskets, and I stared into the grinning face of Lieutenant Lonnie Patrick. I got to my knees and grabbed a handful of underwear.

[92]

"Not really," I said, offended. "I'm fine. My only problem is I happened to have picked a really big fish to fry." I dropped the clothes into one of the baskets. Patrick picked up the M-16 and looked at me, one eyebrow raised.

"Yeah," he said. "But there's your problem. A little fish can't kill a big fish."

"Yes he can," I said. I took the small rifle from him and put it back on top of the clothes, stacked the baskets, and stood up. "He just has to make sure he gets stuck in the big fish's throat."

Patrick opened my car door and I put the clothes on the back seat. "Valid concept," he said. I slipped the pistol from my belt and put it in the glove compartment.

"Lieutenant," I said, "there are going to be a lot of people here in the next few minutes, and they'll be trying to kill me. If you want to chat, then get in your car and follow me." I pushed past him and sat down in my car, cranked it, and put it in reverse. "Are you coming?"

He nodded and ran to his car, cursing me all the way.

TWELVE

We raced to the interstate, and I headed west to the I-10 Trucker's Rest Truck Stop, pulled into the dark, crowded parking lot, and waited for Patrick to get out of his car. We took a booth and I watched the door.

"What the hell did you do this time?" he said.

"Give me a break," I said. "What are you doing here?"

He shrugged. "I took a day off. I've been watching the news, and I had a feeling you were about to do something stupid."

"Well, you're too late," I gloated. "I've already done it."

"Tell me," he said, so I did. When I wrapped up with the details of Katherine's phone call I looked in his big cop face and saw real fear. And concern. I was moved.

"Shit, Clay," he said. "I'm not ready for this. I could handle dirty politics and even radical zealots, but you're talking secret governments and private armies here."

"You're telling me?" I said. "Don't you understand, Lieutenant? This proves Candy's story of the murders at Limestone Creek. That's where they screwed up." He shook his head. The waitress brought burgers and fat, limp fries. Patrick squirted ketchup all over his and ate. I nibbled at mine. "They had to pull them out of there because of it, and they framed poor old Renaldo to cover their asses. And now they know there's a witness."

"You're in a lot more trouble than I can undo," Patrick said, his mouth full. "What now?" I had to trust him. There was no time to play games, and I was too close to the edge to worry about caution. I told him about Mel and his help. I said I was going there to make copies of the videotapes, and I invited him to come along. I called Mel's house, told Torrea I was on the way, and left, belching from the greasy fries.

Torrea and Mel met us at the door, and there was coffee perking in the kitchen. I introduced the lieutenant and quickly summarized the recent events as Mel set up the taping equipment. We took our coffee into the cluttered living room and sat silently watching, first the tape of that night's meeting, then, in awe, the fiery, arrogant oratory of the famous colonel.

It was a stunning tape. A wild tent revival–styled trip into an underworld where everyone outside the small group was either a Communist or an impediment to the American Way. He told them the Contras were an experiment that was being studied by the best intelligence groups for the purposes of not only building an American version but also to decide the methods to be used to ensure public acceptance of them. Whether the Contras ever won a battle wasn't even a concern. The colonel said if the Contras and the Sandinistas killed "everyone in that miserable country," no one would care except for the coffee industry. The audience laughed.

When the tape ended we sat staring at the blank television screen and listened to a whippoorwill calling lonely in the dark night. Torrea was the first to speak. "How?" she said. Mel was hooking up patch cords between tape machines, and he answered without looking up.

"The house bills," he said. "Those four numbers Mac gave me over the phone were the numbers of a house bill. The other three are too. They're designed to join together twenty-three laws already on the books, and they're written so as to reword each just enough to create one new megalaw that'll change the legal system in Florida. I just finished putting it all together in the computer. It will link all law-enforcement agencies in the state and put them under the command of the state government."

"No way!" Lieutenant Patrick almost shouted. "We wouldn't stand for it."

Mel looked at him over the back of the television and smiled sympathetically. "Do you remember PATCO, Lieutenant? The air traffic controllers Reagan replaced early in his administration?" Patrick nodded and looked uneasy. "With the pool of unemployed men in the state, how long do you think it would take to replace you? No offense intended."

"Just imagine," Torrea said, "the media blitz that would go along with it. They could say they were giving those policemen and judges that are soft on drug crimes a chance to back out and save face. They wouldn't be missed, because they'd be replaced by tough new cops who weren't so squeamish."

"And then," Patrick's eyes were cold and hard, "Bob Birk and others like him would form companies that would be licensed to sell drugs legally across the state."

[95]

"And tomorrow, the world," I said. "Holy cow."

Mel made copies and we drank coffee. The ten-o'clock news carried a small story of a brush fire at Limestone Creek. They said it started in a shed filled with illegal fireworks.

After the news, Lonnie Patrick hung around conspicuously until, finally, he spoke up.

"Mr. Shiver," he said. "Clay. I need copies of those tapes. This thing's bigger than you can handle, and it involves me too. I know some people in Tallahassee who carry a lot of weight." He looked at each of us, and I glanced at Mel. "Please."

"Okay," I said. "E pluribus unum, and all that." Mel shrugged and banded two copies together with masking tape. He handed the bundle to Patrick, and Torrea took his free hand in both of hers.

"There are a lot of good people in Florida," she said. "I hope you can find some help. We're going to need it."

I watched the lieutenant drive away and went back inside. Torrea stepped out of a side room with an armload of sheets and pillows, and I followed her down the hall to a small bedroom. We made the double bed, and she opened the window and checked the latch on the screen. "When do you think they'll get here?" she asked quietly, and I said I didn't know.

I was too nervous to stay in one place, so I wandered up and down the hall, watched Mel as he worked at his desk, then stepped out of the house and back into the yard. It was pitch black and at least ten degrees cooler outside. The dogs slipped up and touched their noses to my palm, then, satisfied, drifted away. The whippoorwill still searched for a mate. I walked to the gate and stared down the empty road. The air was still and smelled like dust, and I looked up to a spectacular, starry sky. High above, the tiny red lights of a commercial airliner blinked silently across heaven, and I wondered if Katherine was inside.

When I walked back to the house Mel and Torrea were sitting together on the porch swing, the dogs at their feet.

"Mac," Mel said, "why don't you go ahead and park your car in the barn." I looked at him.

"You'll be staying with us, of course," Torrea said, her arm laced in Mel's, her hand on his cast.

I thought it over and realized I had nowhere else to go, so I spared them the golly-shucks-I'll-just-be-in-the-way stuff and said, "Thank you." I pulled my car into the weathered cypress barn and carried my supplies into the house, spilling the top layer trying to get the baskets out of the back seat. I joined them on the porch and we sat in silence for a long time before Torrea went inside and left Mel and me to mend our fences.

We stumbled over recent events and slowly, painfully, reached back to talk about the past. When he finally talked to me about Patty and the trip he and Torrea made to her funeral, there were tears in his eyes. Torrea brought out a bottle of dry red wine and three glasses, and we drank to the past and the future.

Katherine didn't show up the next day, and by the time it got too dark to work, I had repaired almost every broken thing on Mel's farm. We ate supper late, and I sat up listening to the radio news shows for any scrap of information.

I was up before sunrise, my belt filled with tools and my pockets full of nails, and by nine o'clock in the morning I was filthy and soaked in sweat as Mel and I battled his ancient Allis-Chalmers tractor, muscling the hydraulic unit off in a strange dance of life that resembled Kirk Douglas fighting the giant squid in an old Disney classic. I crawled out from under the tractor when the dogs started barking, and brushed dirt from my arms. A sleek blue BMW rolled through the gate and came to a stop in front of the house. Mel caught up with me when I stopped at the trough to splash water in my eyes. I pulled the tail of my smeared T-shirt up and wiped a clean spot into my face. The dogs stood warily at the doors until Mel shooed them away and Katherine stepped out of the passenger side, a lavender dress swirling around her long legs. A beautiful young woman in jeans and white shirt eased herself from the cool interior of the back seat into the sticky heat. A tall handsome man in a lightweight suit got out of the driver's seat, leaned against the door, and ignored the dogs.

"Mac." Katherine took my hand and laughed at me when I tried to brush off the dirt from the other hand onto my pants leg. "This is Candace, my daughter." The young woman with the chipmunk cheeks looked at me, and I thought she was going to get back in the car. I nodded. Katherine turned me toward the driver.

"This is James," she said. "James Lucas."

There was a tag on the front bumper of the sedan that read "LUCAS-VEGAS BMW." I started to shake hands, looked down at my filthy fingers, and changed my mind. I waved foolishly, and he nodded his head about an eighth of an inch.

James left just before noon the next day, and in the time between, even the minutes were like weeks. After supper, just as the sun dropped behind the thick wall of trees down along the river, he and Katherine went outside and sat on the porch swing. Later, in the darkness, I heard the doors of the BMW open and close. Torrea had driven Mel somewhere to talk to a man about cutting his hay, and Candace stayed in the bedroom and cried.

The house felt smaller than a postage stamp, and I sat in a wooden chair beside the radio, listening as the deejay played every sad song ever written. I woke up on the floor with sunlight in my eyes, and I sat up, listening to the voices in the yard. When I stepped onto the porch, Mel and Torrea were standing just inside the screen door as James said his good-byes to Katherine and Candace. He saw me and called my name, so I walked to the car.

"I want Katherine to live through this," he said.

"So do I." I felt like a kid called to the front of the class to write something a thousand times on the blackboard. That one thing said, he dismissed me and turned to Candy and she ran to him, hugging him as she cried. He pushed her away, nodded at Katherine, then climbed into his car and drove out, hidden from sight by the giant azaleas. Candace darted back into the house and Katherine stared at the gate. I went back to work, but was too clumsy to finish a single project.

Katherine was moody the rest of the day and kept to herself. We said a few things to each other, but they seemed contrived and empty, as though we'd hired poor actors to play our parts and read our lines. Mel and Torrea left again and were gone the rest of the day. When they returned, Mel was fractious and grumbled about friends' not being what they used to be. Somehow that day ended too. Clouds gathered in the afternoon and the humidity built to near one hundred percent, but it didn't rain. Far away, blue-and-yellow lightning crawled across the treetops and thunder rumbled. The air was so heavy that the fireflies stayed at home with their lights off.

The rain came early in the morning and stayed until noon. We sat at the kitchen table, rumpled and haggard and beaten, eyes on our coffee cups. We had the look of front-line veterans in a long war. Torrea nudged us out of our slump by suggesting we think about the other side. "We can be sure they haven't stopped," she said.

Mel asked if I'd made contact with Mark Thornton yet, and I said no. I wanted to be sure Katherine had nothing new to offer first, and she said they hadn't heard anything since word of Dr. Kuyatt's death.

I took Mel's truck down to a small crossroad community some thirty miles from Red Oak and called Mark.

"My God!" he said. "Where are you?" I told him I was calling from a phone booth and that I needed to see him. I suggested a shopping center just off the interstate two exits down and said I'd meet him there at three. I told him I had my proof, and he sounded excited.

We sat on the hood of the truck, and when I told him about the Men's Club, I thought he was going to faint. I handed him copies of the videocassettes and gave him a summary of the contents. He slipped off the truck and walked halfway across the parking lot before he spun around and came back. His lawyer skin actually had sweat on it, and his shirt was soaked.

I told him about Lieutenant Patrick, and his eyes became cartoon circles. "How the hell do you know you can trust him?" he shouted at me, and a woman hurried past with her grocery cart. "Jesus God, Mac," he said, "where is your head? I'm trying to get your ass out of a crack and you're confessing to every stranger on the street!

"Do you even realize you broke a lot of serious laws the other night, and that you voluntarily told a cop about it?" He slammed a soft fist into the truck fender. "Mac, when this is over, I don't want anything more to do with you. At least, not legally."

"Okay." He was strung tightly, and I apologized. He took the bundle I gave him and I filled him in on Katherine and the doctor. He wrote down Mel's phone number but promised he would never call from his office.

Mark raced away in his Mercedes and I wheeled the Trooper toward the plaza exit, then shut it off and closed my eyes. The headache came out of nowhere and ripped through my head like a freight train. I put a hand over my eyes and squeezed my temples. A feeling of resentment toward Katherine surprised me even as it appeared, and before I knew it, I was mad at Sheevers, too. She had left me so permanently and so full of guilt; then Katherine came along and pulled me out of my comfortable seclusion just to bounce me around again. I slapped the dashboard and shouted a profanity at the world.

Why in the hell couldn't they have just left me alone? Why did they both feel the need to involve me in their damned tangled lives, when all I wanted was to skate along into oblivion? When I dropped my hand from my eyes I found myself staring into the rearview mirror. The look of self-pity on my face made me sick. Here I was, feeling sorry for myself while Katherine huddled with her daughter in a stranger's house and watched her world fall apart. I was like the whining husband who says, "It's her fault, not mine. I had to beat her to get her to shut up."

By the time I pulled through the gate to Mel's farm, I had managed to extract my head from my ass. I'd stopped by the grocery store in the little shopping center, and when I carried a bag filled with half gallons of ice cream into the house, I heard the end of the first tape being played. Everyone glanced at me, then turned back to the television. I went into the familiar kitchen, counted out enough bowls for everyone, and passed around the ice cream. Even Candace took one. When the second tape ended, Mel hit the rewind button.

"Mac." Katherine sat beside me on the couch. "Torrea and Mel just told us what happened. You're out of your mind!"

"Thank you," I said. "May I say something?"

"Go ahead," Mel mumbled around a glob of chocolate.

"I almost gave up today," I said. "To tell the truth, I started feeling sorry for myself, and I kept thinking, *Why me?*" I hated this kind of confession. "But it's not me, or even us." I made a circle over their heads with my index finger. "It's going to be everyone if we don't stop them now. These people are evil. I'd like to think they're misguided, but that's not the truth. They're evil, and we can't let them win. This isn't something that will go away."

"Mel said Lieutenant Patrick was with you," Katherine said. I told her about him and said Mark Thornton was worried about my letting Patrick know everything, including where we were.

"That's ridiculous," Katherine said. "I trust him." The telephone rang and Torrea went to answer it as Mel ejected the tape. Torrea called him to the phone, and he came back into the living room slapping his hand against the dirty cast. "That was my friend, Peter Kinsall. I have to get the tractor ready today or he won't be able to get to my fields for another week or two."

"I'll get ready," I said. "We should have the new unit on by supper." I was a little optimistic, but it was ready to run by eight o'clock that night and we'd nailed new two-by-six guides on the trailer by nine. Katherine and Candace had spent the day with Torrea going over all the details of our case.

I took a shower and muttered good night to everyone. The long days of worry and our work on the tractor left me tired, and I suppose I was trying to avoid any more discussion. I didn't even want to think about it.

THIRTEEN

I felt something on my face and I woke with a start. Katherine was sitting on the edge of the bed in a light, sleeveless dress. Her fingers traced my jaw. She smiled. "Let's go for a ride," she said. I blinked at her and tried to wake up. I looked at my watch. It was twelve-thirty, and the quarter-moon in my window was the color of cream. She left the room, and as I sat up and swung my legs over the side I heard her open the front door and step outside. I dressed, and when I stood and reached for my keys, a handful of nails punched my leg through the pocket of my pants.

The night was damp and warmer than it had been. A light fog veiled the moon. I took Katherine's hand and we walked to the barn. She got in my car on the passenger side and I slid in behind the wheel, cranked the car, and backed into the yard. The dogs stood quietly at the gate and moved aside as we went through. We didn't talk.

I tried to remember the road. County-maintained, it had wide ditches on either side all the way to the bend, where the Choctawhatchee River cut a dogleg curve around a piece of high farmland and then shot west again. There, on that bend, was a local swimming hole, and a sandy strip of land ran between a massive oak tree and the river. In the summer, kids parked their trucks in the shade of the oak while they swam. I looked through the thickening fog for the oak. When I came to the first part of the curve I could see its limbs spreading out of the night, though most of its height was lost in the mist. I pulled onto the sandy strip and coasted to a stop. Sounds of the river floated in through the window.

I turned off the engine and looked at Katherine. She came toward me and her hands wrapped my head in a tender web. Her lips attacked mine. She pulled my right hand from the wheel and snaked it around her, easing herself around on the seat until she was lying across my chest. Everywhere we touched was warm. Her hands slipped down my neck to my collar, and her kiss turned serious. I broke free. She raised herself up from my pocket of nails and rubbed her side.

"Katherine," I was already out of breath," I'm not sure—"

"I am." There was anger in her voice. "Now, shut up." Her fingers worked at the buttons of my shirt and her lips left to wander along the side of my face. I felt alarms going off all over, and I began to share her urgency. Suddenly, I became aware of the smell of her hair, the scent of delicate perfume in the soft hollows of her throat, felt the pressure of her breasts as she held us together.

Katherine almost ripped my shirt getting it out of my pants, then she slid off my chest, hooked her fingers in my belt, and said, "Come this way," as she tugged. I squirmed to the middle of the seat and had almost taken a decent drink of air when she kissed me again, this time slowly and passionately. She fumbled with my belt buckle, then unsnapped my jeans, getting the zipper stuck in the process. I pushed her hands away, kicked out of my shoes, and managed to get my pants off while only whacking my head once on the dash and twice on the shifter. She climbed across me, and her white dress floated like a cloud. Her long, cool legs rested against the outside of mine, and she cupped my neck with one hand, curling forward to kiss me as she reached under the dress with the other and held me, guided me to her. Katherine eased down until she was sitting on my lap, and, in total control, she rolled against me in an easy rhythm like a train on a track. I slipped my hands under the light cotton dress and held her waist, and as the gentle force of her lips drew me out, as we explored each other for the right flow, I could have devoured her, breathed her in like a fragrance.

She bit my lip, and when I said, "Ouch," she threw back her head and laughed a husky laugh. It's not that I'd been celibate for five years, but it took that moment for me to realize what a powerful chemical "need" is to the act of making love; the feeling that you want the other person to be glad to be with you. I felt sensations that made me think, *Oh, yeah, now I remember why people go through hell for this.*

After I finished she continued to rock against me slowly, her arms bent, elbows propped upon my shoulders. With her hands on her cheeks she made a tunnel just the size of our faces and we breathed in each other's air, hers like fire on me. Her wet hair was stuck to my temples and her lips brushed my nose as she made a last serpentine thrust that crushed her to me, and I could hear her breathe deeply on my neck. I let my fingers glide down her hips to the soles of her feet, just to let her know I was still alive.

"I think I've been run over by a soft truck," I said, and Katherine kissed my neck. I gathered her dress and lifted it. She pushed back and raised her arms as I slipped it over her head and tossed it in the back. She fell forward and shivered. I wrapped my arms around her and the mist rolled over us, cooling the sweat on our skin. I held her loosely. A single mosquito worked its wings frantically in the wet air in its search for blood, and we ignored it.

"Look in the back seat and see if there are any towels," I said. I thought I remembered spilling some things from the baskets.

"Yes, a couple. Some underwear too." She laughed. "Need some new clothes?" She reached over my shoulder and returned with a pair of jockey shorts with holes in them.

"No," I said, "just the towels." I climbed over her to the door, then dragged her out, lifted her in my arms, and walked toward the river.

"No!" she said, struggling a bit. "No way, Mac!"

It was too late for her to argue as I waded into the cool water, my shirt trailing behind me in the current. I stopped in the chest-deep water, black and swift, and she clung to me, laughing. "My hair!" she said. "Don't let it get wet!" So I lifted her and she wrapped her legs around my waist, my face wedged between her breasts. I kissed her and tried to squeeze water from the ends of her hair.

"Mac, there could be snakes out here," she leaned down and whispered in my ear. "Or alligators."

"You have to trust me, Katherine," I said to her chest. "Remember?"

"Yes," she said. "And I do. I trust you."

Moonlight filtered through the fog just enough for me to get my bearings, and I carried her back to the car, letting her down with a wet slap on the front seat. She reached around the headrest and dug the two towels out of the back. I took one and began fluffing her hair as she unfolded the other and rubbed at me for a few seconds before she started fiddling around.

"Oh-ho!" she said.

"Stop that." I kept working.

"Look who's been brought back to life," she said. I tried to concentrate on her hair, but that soon became impossible.

"Quit," I said. "You're giving mothers all over the world a bad name." I gripped her head in both hands under the towel and pushed her gently back on the seat, then stretched out on top of her. We made love again, slowly.

* * *

[103]

We lay face-to-face on the narrow seat, listening. The water whispered past and pearl-sized drops of dew, gathered from the mist by giant oak limbs, pattered across the roof. Katherine's fingers ran along the small of my back suddenly, and her arm jerked. She rubbed her nose back and forth on my neck.

"Falling asleep?" I asked, and she said, "Yes." She climbed over me to the back seat and came back wearing her dress. I stretched out on the seat and she lay down on top of me. She snickered.

"What?" I said.

"Nothing, really," she said. "I was just thinking."

"Tell me." Her legs slid down my sides and she crossed her arms on my chest, then propped her chin up in the vee. My eyes closed, I could feel her breath on my lips.

"I was thinking of the look on your face when we drove up," she said.

"Oh."

"No, no!" she said earnestly. "You don't understand. I was so happy to see you. I honestly felt like I was home." Her thick hair fell forward in a cascade. "It was nice."

"I felt like Pepino," I said. "I thought you were going to ask for my green card." She laughed and squeezed me with her thighs.

"My father was a mechanic," Katherine said. "He worked on school buses in the county shop every day. He even died there." She stopped and put her cheek against her arm.

"Every day he came home smelling like oil and grease and cleaning solvents." Her voice was far away. "I used to wait hours for him. He'd pick me up and hug me, and I loved him so. He was the kindest man I've ever known," she said. "You won't scare me away with dirt." Her voice was deep and vibrated on my chest.

"You know, Mac," she said. "You're very good at what you do." She hesitated, and it sounded as if maybe she'd crawled out on her own little limb. "There are a lot of people in Las Vegas who would hire you. People who wouldn't try to get you killed."

"Well, I can't leave right now," I mumbled. "I mean, there are so many things I need to do here in Palmetto Bay. And I have the house, and all . . ." She didn't move for several seconds.

"What?" She lifted her head, and her eyes narrowed.

"My house." I was getting uncomfortable. "I . . . I have a lot of things unfinished, you know?" Katherine put her hand flat on the center of my chest and pushed herself slowly to a sitting position. She

[104]

leaned down, staring into my eyes. Her face was rock-still and her palm was hot.

"Goddamn you," she said, then she slapped me so hard it burned. She slapped me again.

"Wait—" I said, and caught her wrist as she swung the third time.

"Goddamn you!" Katherine twisted free, pushed herself backward, and bolted from the car. I sat up and fumbled for my pants, pulled them from the floor, and struggled into them, poking another hole in my leg. When I stepped from the open door I saw her standing with her back to me in thigh-deep water, her white dress billowing around her like the opened petals of a morning glory. It spun lazily, wrapping itself around her legs.

"Katherine," I said, stepping to the water's edge.

"Stay away from me!" she said. "What do you think I'm made of, you son of a bitch? Rubber, maybe?" She turned, and in the dim gray dawn, her exquisite form drew light from the horizon. She seemed to glow. "Katherine Furay, the unbreakable woman?"

"Hey," I raised my hands, "I just want you to understand—"

"Shut up!" she shouted across the space between us. "Don't you think I understand, Mac? Patty Sheevers was my best friend. She never let me down my whole life," Katherine said. "She swiped her dad's car and drove me to the hospital the night Candace was born. You ask me to understand, when it's you, damn it. It's you that doesn't understand."

She looked at me, angry and hurt. "Patty's dead. I'm alive, and I want you because I like who you are. But I don't sympathize with you, Mac." She walked out of the water, but kept her distance from me.

"If you loved her, if you respected Patty," she said, "you'd let her go. Don't you see, you've turned her into your ideal woman, your centerfold. Her opinions are your opinions, her wants and desires are always the same as yours. That's not real."

"Katherine," I said in protest, "I made an oath to Sheevers."

"You made an oath to yourself," she said, suddenly weary of the argument. "Patty is gone, and I will not resent her, damn you!" Birds woke in the trees and, far away, a peacock screamed.

"I want a commitment from you, Mac," she said. "I'm not talking about wedding bells and a little house in the country. I mean a commitment to try, because I didn't leave James for you. I did it for me, for the same reason I made love with you last night. It felt good to do that, to fuck because I wanted to, and not because I felt an obligation.

[105]

"I'm a living woman, and I might do things that really piss you off. I might have opinions and habits that you don't like, but I'm real, McDonald Clay, and Patty's not, not anymore." She shook her head and walked up the bank past my car, leaned against the big oak, and closed her eyes. I turned to the river and watched the day begin.

Two therapists spent almost a year trying to exorcise her from me, but I had carved a Sheevers-sized hole in my heart and, like a junkie, I loved my fix. Katherine's words hurt deep and I wanted to ignore them, but I sat on the sand and thought about what she'd said. The sky turned a citrus yellow, then, very slowly, a deep blue.

I heard a rustling sound behind me, and Katherine made a silly noise. When I stood and turned back to her, prepared to change, ready to laugh, I saw her being lifted into the air by two large men in jungle fatigues. One held a hand over her mouth, his other arm around her waist. The second man struggled with her thrashing legs. I leapt forward, but someone knocked me down and it felt as though a piano was dropped on my back.

A pair of arms gripped me in a vise, and whoever it was had biceps larger than my thighs. A pointed chin dug into my neck, and I could smell the hyped-up breath of an ugly man. I tried to twist away, but his hands were locked onto his thick-veined forearms. He lifted me to my toes.

"Take your hands off her!" I said stupidly. Someone laughed, and the man who held Katherine's face in his hand unsnapped a large knife from his belt with the other and lifted it to her tender throat. Time screeched to a halt as she looked helplessly at me.

"Not yet." It was a voice that sounded familiar, but when he stepped into view I didn't recognize him immediately. He wore camouflaged fatigues with red epaulets and a red brim on his flat-topped cap. I'd noticed the soldier at the Men's Club had gold epaulets and trim; these wore dark green. One, a tall, gaunt soldier who trailed the man with the red brim, had gold stripes on his epaulets and I figured it must be a form of rank, since they wore none on their sleeves and had no insignia. Thinking of the Men's Club made me remember this man. The speaker behind the podium.

"She stays alive until we have her daughter," he said. The gorilla held my arms tightly, but no one had thought to shut my mouth.

"You guys seem to be big on attacking women," I said. "How can you make an army out of a bunch of sissies?" I thought it best to keep the conversation simple. The speaker walked over to me, and I saw a gold star on his collar.

"So you're McDonald Clay?" He didn't ask it as a question to be answered. "Good. It will be nice to eliminate you before we kill her daughter." Katherine shouted into the man's hand, and I thought of Mel and Torrea asleep, of Candace alone.

"I saw you at the Men's Club," I said. "You're the moron that wants to take over the world."

"So," he said, "it *was* you!" He leaned in close. "Then it will be a pleasure killing you. Stanley is in the hospital because of you."

"War is hell," I quoted another general.

"Stanley is my son," he said indignantly. I thought of his willingness to go after someone else's daughter.

"Good," I said. "Now you're a matched set. Neither one of you has any balls." He punched me in the stomach, but I was so numb by that time from the giant's grip on my chest that I didn't even feel it. I laughed at him. I prayed to God for any good idea, but got a dial tone in reply. I figured it was a little late in my life to remember Him, and God might be wary of any conversion of mine made under duress. The man holding Katherine offered his knife to the general. He thought it over.

"No," he said. He looked past me to the goon with the bad breath and grinned. "Drown him."

"Mac!" Katherine tore free from the hand and cried out, but the man captured her again. She fought against the two of them.

"Put her in the car," the general said, and they took her away. He winked at Bruno. "You'll enjoy this, Sergeant. When it's over, come to the farm." He walked out of my line of sight and hulk spun me around, showing me the river. I strained against his hold, but I don't think he even noticed. He chuckled. I felt the water work its way up my pants legs as he moved easily into deeper water. Retuning his steel grip across my chest, he prepared me for baptism.

My feet were off the bottom, and I watched a small twig float by under my chin as the soldier pushed me down. I quickly filled my lungs with all the air I could get in the small space he left me. My head went under and I closed my eyes, then opened them again in the murky water. I fought but was no match for him, and a bubble of air escaped my lips, a little glob of my soul headed toward heaven.

I put my feet against his shins and pushed, kicked slowly in the thickness of the river, but couldn't move him. Another bubble popped out and my chest started to hurt. It felt as if one more set of arms were squeezing above his. My body was burning the oxygen from my lungs and less was making it up the road to my brain. I thought I saw the sun, but the illusion passed and the water around my face was turning black. I fought to keep my mouth closed and felt myself weaken. A tunnel of bright light appeared in a perfect circle just inside the door of my mind, and I looked down it for Sheevers. This was the moment I'd waited for; five years of planning, and there was no one there. A little bubble of expended gases leaked from my lips, and I knew without a doubt that Patty wasn't coming for me. She hadn't been there, just as I wouldn't be there for Katherine. I got mad.

Kong was getting bored, and his grip loosened as I stopped fighting him. I swung my hand onto my leg and felt something in my pocket. Little white fireworks were going off in my head as I pulled one of the long galvanized nails from the pocket and reached out of the water, flailing a partially closed fist lightly against his head until I found his ear. I grasped it tenderly, like a baby, and he didn't pull away. The nail slipped once as I worked it across my palm, but I held on to it, pushed the tip into his ear, and, with the last bit of strength I could find, slammed it home with the heel of my palm.

He roared and lifted me from the water. I sucked in a burning lungful of air, knocked his arms back, and twisted around to face him. He really was ugly, and his face was contorted in pain as his thick fingers dug for the nail's head. I slapped the hand and he screamed, his other hand coming out of nowhere with a razor-sharp knife that flashed past my face and cut a thin line along the top of my forearm. I put my feet on his belt and pushed away, heading for the bank, but I stumbled and fell flat on my back in the shallower water.

Blood oozed from his ear and his head hung sideways as he staggered after me, the knife slashing diagonal arcs in the wind. I stood up and dug my toes into the muddy river bottom. I hoped he wouldn't connect with the next swing and I dodged under his arm, came up on the inside, and brought my palm solidly onto his ear with a wet slap. His mouth opened wide and his eyes rolled back, the hand holding the knife hanging between us. I slapped again, and he stumbled. My hand snaked over his wrist, and I turned the large knife around until the point bent the fabric of his shirt.

I pushed off from the mud and slammed hard into the handle, driving the blade into his chest until we were locked together in an obscene dance. His eyes closed and then reopened halfway. He stared at me as he slipped into the moving water, tangling around my legs. I kicked at his body until we separated and I watched him drift in the flow, making a lazy turn to end up lying sideways just under the surface, one blind eye staring up at nothing. The knife flashed once in the morning sun as the current rolled him away.

I crawled onto the clay bank and stayed on my hands and knees, gasping for air. I wanted to lie down and sleep, to close off this world, but I heard automatic-weapons fire in the distance. I shook my head and tried to pull myself together. The cut on my arm wasn't bad, but my body couldn't keep making new blood to replace what I was losing, so I tore off my shirt and wrapped it around the cut. It seemed as if I'd never make it to the car, but I did somehow. Someone came roaring down the road, and I crouched behind my car trunk. A big black Lincoln with dark tinted windows raced by in a cloud of red dust, and I couldn't see who was inside. They didn't slow down. Katherine was in there, surely, and Candace might be too.

I jumped in my car, and the keys were still dangling from the ignition. I cranked up and almost followed the limo, but another rapid round of popping fire reminded me of my priorities. I couldn't abandon Mel.

FOURTEEN

My car dug twin trenches in the red clay as it spun around, and the steering wheel fought against my hands. I reached into the glove compartment, pulled out the pistol, and checked its clip. I dropped it beside me on the seat and dug around until I found the spare clip. I looked it over and pushed it into my pocket.

I made a clumsy high-speed turn at the gate, and when the car clipped one of the thick creosoted posts, my pistol zipped across the seat and fell between it and the door. I could hear the sharp crack of Mel's 30.06 and saw three soldiers running in a crouch from the barn toward the house, firing on the run. The kitchen window shattered. I stomped the gas pedal to the floor and bounced across the yard, hitting the first runner solidly with the left fender as the other two scattered. When I stepped on the brake pedal, the wheel spun out of my hands and the car skidded sideways.

It would have flipped over, but it hit the water trough and shuddered to a stop in a billowing cloud of dust. I scrambled over the seat and dug for the pistol, found it wedged halfway under, and kicked open the door. Just as my feet hit the ground I heard bullets impacting in the rear and I dropped into a prone position, trying to see through the dirt. He was shooting right at me but they were going high, punching holes in my car at least a foot over my head, so I stayed where I was, steadied my pistol, and waited.

When a breeze whipped the dust away suddenly he was straight in front of me, and I dropped him with one shot. I dug in and looked for the second man but heard only the clicking sounds of the engine as it cooled. My eyes swept the side yard slowly and I saw the soldier I ran down lying in a heap just inside the cattle crossing. I stood cautiously and walked to the man in front of me, picked up his M-16, from the dirt, and, in a crouch, spun until I saw the third man. The first soldier must have been thrown into him as I sped by, and he, in turn, knocked

[110]

into the barbed-wire fence with enough force to pull two fenceposts from the earth. The wire was wrapped around him in a tight and deadly tangle, and he stared at me silently, helplessly, as I ran past him to the house.

The world was quiet, but, by the carnage in Mel's front yard, I knew it had been a hell of a fight. The bodies of Sack-o and Van Zeti lay in a tangle of three dead soldiers at the pecan tree, and two more men had fallen just inside the line of azaleas. Hanging through the torn screen of Mel's front porch where we'd sat so many times, drinking iced tea and arguing, was the soldier who'd held the knife to Katherine's throat. By the look of his face and chest, he must have caught both barrels of a shotgun at fairly close range. These ersatz soldiers in this new army seemed long on macho but, fortunately, short on experience, the one element that allows you to act on instinct. I didn't want to see what happened inside, but I couldn't put if off any longer. I stopped at the front door and lifted the pistol, then called out. "Mel?" I said. "Torrea?" Nothing. A cat growled in fright from under the porch.

"Mel?" I listened for any sound. "It's me. McDonald Clay." I heard something moving toward the door, and I stepped to the side of the porch, pistol ready.

"McDonald?" I heard Torrea whisper. "Is that really you?"

I dropped the pistol to my side and discarded the M-16, then raced up the steps to where Torrea stood in a well-worn cotton gown, its faded patterns spattered with blood. She leaned on a twelve-gauge shotgun and her hand was bloody. I stepped inside and put my arm around her. "Melvin's in here," she said. We walked to the kitchen where the bearlike old man lay between the table and the shattered window, his striped pajama top stained red. Torrea broke from me and knelt beside him, cradling his head in her plump arms. She looked into his sleepy eyes, then up at me.

"This is what men do?" she said. "Why, McDonald? It's so stupid. So stupid." She kissed Mel's forehead.

"Mac?" His voice was like the wind. "Help Patricia, Mac. They'll kill her. Help her!" I looked from him to Torrea.

"He's been calling Candace 'Patricia' since the shooting started," she said. "He sent her out back earlier and told her how to get to the boat landing, but I just saw some men going that way." She looked at Mel, at her hand.

"I'll be all right, McDonald," she said, "and there's nothing you can do for Melvin. He's always loved you, you know." I felt tears of frustration, of rage.

"Save Candace," Torrea said. "Do what you can, McDonald. I want to be alone with Melvin now." I touched her cheek with my fingers, then ran out the back door to the crest of the hill that overlooked Mel's beautiful land. It was bordered by the river as it made its casual turn through lush hardwoods and fertile farmland, then stretched out on its push to the west.

I resisted the temptation to run toward the landing and, instead, stopped and let my eyes take in the landscape. I had been taught well by veterans who survived because they, too, had learned. The clumps of oaks and sprinklings of pines fell into a pattern of lines and colors, and I waited, watching, until I saw a flash of white once, then twice between trees along the bottomland. Candace was running the wrong way, away from the boats.

Several hundred yards west of Candace, two men crept toward her, but I don't think they knew she was there. Their arrogant moves negated the camouflage they wore. As I ran toward a middle ground I watched the tree line on either side and, almost too late, I saw two more men just as they came out of a thicket just behind the young woman. I cut across the clearing above them, and as one grabbed the back of her thin white gown and reached for her hair, I stopped, steadied myself, and shot him.

I guess it was just poor aim, because he went down and came back up, so instead of being able to concentrate on the other guy, I was divided and they both shot back. I took out the second man before I emptied my clip, but by the time I slipped in the spare and cocked the pistol, Candy had run off into the woods toward the slough. The first soldier, his pants leg turning red at the thigh, was limping along behind her. The other two were shouting questions from the far end like idiots. I wouldn't want them backing me up in a firefight.

I knew the land sloped down to the east, so I took a chance and headed that way, hoping she'd run downhill and not up. I crashed through a titi thicket and literally wound up on top of them. Candy was on her back in a clump of wire grass, and the soldier was sitting on her chest with his hands around her throat. His pants leg was drenched in blood, and he had a lost look in his eyes. Candy was fighting him, and as I raised the pistol and pointed it at his face I heard her gasp, not in pain but in terror, her eyes locked on the gun. I couldn't do it.

I kicked at him and he deflected my foot, so I stomped his bloody

[112]

leg, then kicked him. This time it worked and he fell from Candace, gripping his thigh and grunting. I pulled her to her feet and half dragged her back toward the landing. As we closed in on the riverbank she stumbled, and when I reached to steady her, I saw her bare feet and legs were ripped from the blackberry thickets. She hadn't said a word. I picked her up and ran, out of shape and wheezing, and I heard the other men firing from a distance. The terrain was rough along the bank, and I was having trouble with my footing. It seemed as though every step was uphill.

I tried to skid down the bank on my heels but lost my balance and spun, hitting the water with her on top of me. I'd had enough of water, but we would never beat them to the landing, and Mel's boat engines were in about the same shape as his tractor had been. I gathered her up and reversed my direction, working back upstream toward the soldiers and listening for them. My eyes felt as if they were full of sand, and I kept blinking as I searched the bank, peering under each big tree until I found what I wanted.

There, behind the tall grasses in the dark mud, was a black hole between a mass of thick roots and vines. A place where the river had gotten a toehold and dug patiently, sifting dirt and pebbles and carrying them away. Eventually, the big tree would ease down until it touched the swift river and someone would spend a long, miserable day cutting it up and getting it out of the way. That, however, was in the future. At the moment, it seemed a perfect place to hide.

I gripped one of the roots and eased Candace through the wet opening. Holding her waist, I guided her into the muddy black cavern, musky and deep. The river's movement was a dull rumble, and ripples of light danced and sparkled, dazzling in the darkness.

"Oh, you're bleeding," Candace said. I thought she was talking about my forearm, but she touched above the dirty, wrapped shirt, and when her fingers met my left shoulder it felt as if she had set me on fire. When my eyes adjusted to the dim light I glanced down at an angry red hole in my shoulder and turned slowly from her.

"What does it look like back there?" I asked, and she touched it gingerly.

"The same, I guess," she said.

"Good." I faced her again. "It went through." There wasn't time to consider the negative consequences, and, besides, I'd always been a good healer, a pack mule. I ground my teeth as she used the hem of her gown to wet the bleeding wound with warm river water.

"Where's my mother?" she said.

"They have her."

"No!" It was a devastating sound.

"She's safe," I said, "as long as you are."

"Oh, God," Candace said. She pulled herself into a sitting position in the shallow water and I lost my balance, plopping down in front of her and soaking us both again. I had tried to keep the pistol dry, but it was wet by the time I shook it and wedged it between two dangling roots.

"What happened to the Shivers?" she asked, and I told her. She sighed. She pulled my head into her lap and covered my shoulder with the gown, dipped water with her cupped hand, and sprinkled it over the wound. I felt dizzy.

"My mother is in love with you," Candace said.

"I love her too," I mumbled. A dull pain spread down my fingers and up into my neck. She didn't say anything else, so I closed my eyes and felt the rhythmic flow of water over me as she dipped and poured. Dipped, poured.

"Are they going to kill her?" she said at last. I shook off the darkness of sleep and, groggy, shook my head.

"No," I said. "It won't happen, Candace. Katherine is a survivor. You are too," I added. "That's why you're here with me now. That's why you made it home alive the night your friends were murdered." Her hand stopped dipping and the throbbing fire returned.

"I shouldn't have," she said. "I should've done something. I just watched it happen." Her hand began dipping and pouring again.

"If I had died there, none of this would be happening." Candace almost whispered the words. "My mother would be safe now."

"Uh-uh," I muttered into the silky material stretched over her thigh. "She wouldn't be the same woman. Besides, you can't play those kinds of games, pal. I've been doing it for years. Your mom finally convinced me that life goes on." We both heard the shouting, and her hand gripped the back of my neck. We sat very still, and I twisted my head around enough to see the dripping pistol. I raised my sore arm and pulled the gun to me, then fell back between her legs, my head on her stomach, the pistol against my chest.

Someone was splashing through the water and coming steadily closer. Two men came in view between the tangle of roots. They walked within ten feet of us, cursing us for making their lives difficult. When their noises faded, Candace said, "Dying would be better than this."

"No way," I said. "You don't believe that and neither do I. You feel

[114]

guilty because you couldn't save your friends, and I've been doing the same thing with Sheevers.

"Katherine's doing the same about you," I continued. "Who knows, maybe everyone in the world's going through the same crap. But dying's worse, and don't forget it.

"I'm going to tell you something I've never told anyone." I pulled my arm tightly to my side and lifted myself out of the water, stood unsteadily, then dropped down beside her. She was shaking, and I put my good arm around her shoulders. "I was in a place one time where everyone died but me. All I remember of the first part was a lot of bright lights, then I was lying in the mud with a bone sticking out of my leg. I didn't know where I was until I looked around and saw all those dead men. People were screaming and the explosions kept on, just like someone walking around stepping on ants. I was so scared, I begged God to let me die too." I leaned back slightly and remembered.

"There were people shooting everywhere, and I stood up in the middle of it, squeezed my eyes shut, and started begging God to not let it hurt. I stood there like a dope and nobody shot me. When I finally got my panic under control and decided I wanted to live, I got shot. Twice." I could still feel the dead spots on my left side, still remember dragging a broken leg across a nasty piece of mountainside.

"I made up my mind then. Nothing was going to stop me from getting back, from going home." I stopped and listened, but could hear only the sounds of the river. Candace was still shaking, but not as bad. "I covered myself with mud and sticks and leaves and turned into a troll, waiting for someone to come by on this little path I found—covered everything except my hands. I stayed there all night, and in the morning, when it was still dark, a man came by and I killed him. I ate his measly food and I took his little pouch full of pills, and then I waited until another man came, and I did it again. It took me a week to find my way back to my own lines, and what I did, I did to survive.

"I thought Sheevers's death was the end of my life, but it wasn't. We're going to get Katherine back from those bastards, Candy." Here I was, bullshitting again. "I want you to stay under here and make a long list of all the things you want to do and see in your life. I'm going back now to find a way out of here for the two of us."

It had always been my favorite game when I was a kid. I even got in trouble sometimes just to see if I could get back out. Call me irresponsible. There were quite a few times that it didn't work. "You're going to get lonely and scared, and then you're going to start thinking something bad happened and that I'm not coming back, but don't believe it. I'll be back before dark. I need you, and so does Katherine.

"Wait for me," I said. She nodded, and I thought, *God she looks like her mother.*

"Mac." She even sounded like her. I looked back. "I promised myself I wouldn't like you," she said. "But you're okay."

"Thanks," I said, and when I turned back around to wade through the roots, a searing pain ripped through my shoulder and headed straight for my brain. The last thing I saw as I blacked out was bubbles of air coming out of my nose, and I thought, *Oh, no, not again.*

FIFTEEN

It was a long and lousy night. I don't know where the day went, only that it was night and it lasted forever. I spent the entire time drowning. Water poured through my nose and my mouth, flowed through my ears. And even though the water was ice cold, I was burning like a log in a fire. I thrashed around like a madman trying to breathe, but every time I made it to the surface, Candace made me eat rocks until I sank again.

Candace had become a monster, and I hated her. I feared and loathed her. She was dressed in black now, like the Vietminh, and her grinning face leaned close to mine in the darkness. I begged her to help me, but she pried open my mouth each time and poured rocks down my throat until I went back under.

When daylight came I was still in the crackling fire, and its harsh smoke stung my nostrils. Water still surrounded me. I could hear it gurgling, and when I put my hand to my face, the water poured from me. I was terrified. It kept getting hotter and hotter, and I felt the flesh peeling away from my bones, layer by layer, until I sat up and put a hand over my racing heart.

"Mac?" Candace had been standing beside me, looking through the tall pines, and she looked down, her face lined and impossibly pale. She knelt and put a cold hand on my face. I drew back.

"No more rocks!" I said, and she wiped my neck and shoulders with a cool, wet cloth. She wore a dark-blue knit shirt and jeans, with worn white Reeboks on her feet. Her dark hair was pulled back and held with a navy-blue ribbon. I stared at her angrily until the visions of the night faded and reality stepped in with a bag full of questions. She didn't give me the chance to ask any.

"They're burning Mr. Shiver's house," Candace said sadly. "It's almost over now." I saw ugly gray trails of smoke drifting over me, and tried hard to pull things together.

"Please," I said, "start over. Where did you get those clothes? Where are we? What time is it?" She never stopped dipping the cloth into a bowl of water and wiping the sticky sweat from my upper body. She looked older than Torrea.

"We're on the riverbank," she said. "Beside the tree we were hiding under. I almost didn't get you up here." I thought of her struggling with an unconscious man in the water, somehow getting me up that rugged bank. There were scrapes and bruises on her arms, and I was embarrassed that I'd been hating her. She looked at her watch.

"It's seven-thirty A.M., and you've been out since yesterday morning." I tried to comprehend that. "Yesterday afternoon I decided to go to Mr. Shiver's house to get clothes and medicine and stuff—"

"Wait a minute!" I said. "You went back?" She nodded. "Jesus, Candy, weren't you afraid they'd catch you?"

"Mac," she said, "I have to tell you. If anyone had been within a mile of us yesterday, they would've found us easily. You've been yelling and talking nonstop for just about eighteen hours."

"Really?" I felt I should be wearing a clown suit. I wanted to ask what I'd said, but I was afraid she'd tell me.

"I found Mr. Shiver's box of medicine and I brought it back with me." She reached down and lifted a cardboard box into view. I looked around us at a small collection of food, clothing, and medications.

"I did what you said." She shifted her eyes from me, "Sort of. I became a troll—I took off my gown and covered myself with mud from the bank there," she said, pointing. "I went a little way each time, then I sat still and watched, and it worked. There were two men at the gate, but I didn't see anyone in the yard or house, so I went inside and grabbed a bunch of stuff.

"I've been cramming antibiotics down you for about twelve hours. I came to the conclusion that I really had nothing to lose and you're the only one who can get me out of here. I don't even know where I am."

My mouth was hanging open. I took the cloth from her hand and wiped my face, took stock, and decided I was going to live. "I still can't believe you got me out of the water," I said.

"It wasn't easy," she said. Looking into her eyes was like seeing Katherine, except Katherine's eyes were filled with anger, Candy's with fear.

"I thought you were feeding me rocks," I said. I put the cloth back down. "I thought I was drowning. Help me to my feet." Candace wrapped my good arm around her and strained to lift me as I stood on new legs, boneless and weak. She walked me to the edge of the strip of hardwoods, and I could see the billowing smoke from Mel's house. I sat down. My arm was wrapped in gauze and tape, and though it hurt, it was usable. We ate most of the food she'd brought, and I washed myself off and put on the clothes she'd collected from my baskets. She also brought the box of ammunition.

"I thought those were the ones for your gun," she said. My pistol was lying on a folded blouse and looked clean and dry. The clip lay beside it. I filled it and slipped it into place.

"Is it ever going to stop?" Candace said.

"I promise you," I told her, "I'll do everything I can to finish this, Candy. I do love Katherine, and I'm scared for her, too. I really believe I can get her out of this, but I'm going to need your help all the way through." She nodded, and I looked into eyes that were as worn out as they were beautiful. The tree I leaned against was warm and solid against my back, and I needed time to think. I pulled her over and she was too far gone to protest, asleep before her cheek settled on my thigh. I munched on cookies and rubbed her back lightly, remembering Mel Shiver and hoping Torrea was safe somewhere. No one seemed safe. The normal rules of playing politics between the forty-yard lines was out and the fanatics were making a run for the end zone. I had serious doubts as to what we'd accomplished, and as much as I tried to avoid it, I thought of Katherine. I had a hard time believing she was still alive.

Here, sleeping beside me, was the nice daughter of a very nice woman, and they were both going through hell because a handful of powerful fools believed they had a better plan for running the world. I didn't know how to stop them. Several hours slipped by as I came up with new ideas and plans, only to cancel each of them. I still refused to admit that Lieutenant Patrick turned us in to these rodents, but I didn't know where else to take it. Katherine told me the day James left that he had made plans to drive to New Orleans and lie low until this thing was over.

I slipped out from under Candace and let her head down gently on a stack of clean clothes. Mel kept his truck in the barn, because, since his broken leg, they'd used Torrea's car. He'd asked me to drive it to meet Mark that day just to make sure the battery hadn't run down. It occurred to me that it might have been overlooked. I had put it back there after my trip, and Mel kept a spare key in his workbench. The fact that they burned his home might mean they were abandoning the search for us at Mel's. I guessed they were shouting at each other a lot.

[119]

Bob Birk was probably sweating tiny bullets, because I was sure he'd convinced them he was without blemish when they chose him to be the leader of this new world.

Before I made the trip to the barn I drew a map of the surrounding roads and wrote down a few phone numbers of people who might be willing to help Candy if I didn't make it back. I placed it beside her and used the box of ammunition for a paperweight.

There wasn't a soul anywhere, not even curious neighbors, but they'd be around soon if the soldiers were gone. I didn't have much time. The barn door was closed, and it opened noisily. I knew it would, but I wanted to make a racket. If there were any of the general's boys anywhere nearby, I wanted them to find me before I brought Candace out of hiding. Nothing stirred. The key was in its box, and when I cranked the Trooper, it fired up instantly. The gas needle showed almost a full tank. I dropped the pistol into the pocket on the driver's-side door and turned off the ignition. When I stepped out and shut the door behind me, a figure appeared in the open barn doors.

"Don't ever leave me alone again, Mac," Candace said, her arms full of supplies. "Not ever. Not until we get Mom back."

"Okay," I said. "Sorry."

They'd left my car where it slammed into the trough, and I retrieved my shoes. There was still a dark circle beside the cattle crossing surrounded with scatterings of clipped barbed-wire fencing. These people were paying dearly for their mistakes. They weren't soldiers. They were that terrible mutation that comes from believing in your own propaganda. The kind of officer that allows his troops to blast heavy-metal rock music at a church embassy; the kind of soldier that follows only the laws he agrees with.

Real soldiers are ethical, in spite of the nature of their jobs. Or perhaps because of it. That's why the chain of command is so important in the military. It's a strong rope that binds the bottom to the top and gives the foot soldier a purpose to do what needs to be done and the knowledge that he's following a well-worn path. These men were vigilantes, and they would only get worse.

I thought of Mel as I drove slowly from his ravaged farm, of the irascible old fart who believed in things I couldn't comprehend, who upheld the most liberal of theories. I used to shake my head in wonder as he tried to share his visions of the world with me. The difference was, his beliefs were based on lifelong convictions, not thirty-second sound bites. When you pulled them apart to see how they worked, there was something inside.

I didn't agree with Mel very often, but I always respected him. The world changed with his death. These men were different, in my eyes. They were the tares between the wheat. Mel told me once that what made us Americans wasn't our laws but our attitudes, that laws are just a reflection of the attitudes. I tried to imagine Florida under these new laws that were even now slipping quietly through the legislature, being readied to be passed unnoticed by a bored and jaded club. I couldn't imagine it.

I drove uneasily down the dirt road, past the bend where Katherine and I had spent the night. Candace rode silently, and I could feel her eyes on me, another stranger controlling her destiny. After we left the clay road behind and eased smoothly over the blacktop, she leaned on the window and slept. I ate another handful of antibiotics, and as the lush countryside passed in a blur, I thought of Katherine.

Bob Birk's sordid past was costing his backers a fortune, and I knew that didn't make them happy, but I got no pleasure from it, either. She had been taken from me, and I wanted her back. Alive. Mel was dead, and I didn't know where Torrea was. There was still no place in my mind where I could find shelter, no road signs for me. I was lost, and there was at least one person still alive who needed me. As I watched her in the stillness of sleep I wished the burden were on someone else. I prayed again to my neglected God.

It was hard to believe that Lonnie Patrick turned us in, but I didn't want to think Mark would, either. Someone had let them know where we were. I slipped the Trooper into a parking space in the crowded shopping center across the street from Barret, Barret and Finch, the law firm that Mark called home. A dull-gray box of architectural arrogance, rescued from the ordinary by the line of expensive cars in front and a heavy blue surf that roared a hundred yards beyond. Happy, unconcerned people frolicked in the sand. Children built castles and young men and women turned a golden brown. Just a few miles up the road, Mel Shiver's house had been burned to the ground, and somewhere in the river, a dead man was bouncing along with a knife in his chest.

Political zealots were getting ready to turn Florida into an experiment of truly despotic proportions, and either I was crazy for worrying about it, or these people were insane for not paying attention. I listened to the music playing softly on the radio while Candace slept, and when my eyes drifted down her long, slender forearms I was shocked to see a double line of ugly white scars, dimpled with stitch marks and stark against her brown wrists.

[121]

They weren't the hesitant scratches of someone looking for sympathy, but the healed lips of deeply sliced skin, the signs of someone who had intended to check out for good. I thought of how she saved my life, and I was humbled. My grief had for years elevated me above those around me as I convinced myself that only I had truly suffered.

When the top-of-the-hour local news came on the radio, the lead story was of yesterday's shoot-out at the home of a long-suspected drug kingpin, and reported the deaths of four DEA agents during the raid of Mel's heavily armed fortress. The newsman said that Torrea Shiver was under protective custody because of fears of retaliation from the smuggling ring, hinting she was the one who, suffering from guilt, had turned her husband in to the authorities.

A strange undercurrent was there, however; one I hadn't seen before in the case. The reporter read all the words in their proper order, but there was a sound of disbelief, of a dubious tale. He practically made fun of the story. I suddenly found energy, and, restless, I dug around in Mel's truck, looking for a quarter for the pay phone. I searched the glove compartment, then the box between the seats. Candace stirred, then sat up quickly, staring at me with furrowed brows. I saw the wildness then. The cold, frightening glimpse into a dark and lonely soul, and I could see how close to the line she was, knew how tenuous the hold she kept on herself. I could be the catalyst that kept her on one side or pushed her to the other.

She blinked, rubbed her eyes with curled fingers, and looked around at the bright sand and busy street. Our nerves were raw and we were running on adrenaline, not the best thing for our mental health, not to mention decision making.

"Do you have any money?" I said as she grappled with the reality of waking to a hostile world.

"I don't know," Candace said. She fumbled in the bag she'd brought with her. She held up my bankroll. "I have this. Why? Do you want to buy some whiskey?"

"God, no," I said, stripping a ten from the roll and handing the rest back. "I'm depressed enough already." I got out of the truck and stretched, careful not to jiggle my left arm. I walked to the grocery store and bought orange juice and a couple of packs of gum, then sidled up to the pay phone and called Mark on his personal number. He answered on the second ring.

"Mac?" He was startled, and I waited while he fumbled for words. "Sweet Jesus, Mac, I thought you were dead!"

"I am," I said. "Booga-booga."

[122]

Candace was watching me from the truck, and I looked at her pretty face, thought of Birk's abuses, and felt another stirring of anger. "Mark, I need some answers—"

"Wait!" He sounded scared. "Just wait!" He put me on hold. I stood first on one foot and then the other. My shoulder hurt, and I wondered how Candace had stuffed her swollen feet into the Reeboks. I cursed lawyers. When the phone clicked in my ear it wasn't Mark on the line. I hung up, dropped in a quarter, and dialed again.

"Mr. Clay." It was the voice from the old dental-hygiene films. "Please don't hang up. I'm Inspector Prossett of the Federal Bureau of Investigation."

"You have thirty seconds," I said, trying to remember how much time it took to trace a call. For all I knew, they could do it instantly. "Talk to me."

"Good enough," he said. "The bottom line is that General Hart and his troops were arrested today by federal agents. Katherine Furay is safe and she is with my people." My knees turned to rubber.

"We're afraid her daughter has been murdered," he said. "Miss Furay is taking it very hard." I made a quick decision.

"Her daughter is with me," I said. "We're at the north end of the county now, but we'll head for the beach. We should be there in thirty minutes or so, depending on traffic." I hung up, then called again.

"Don't come here," the man said. "We have made a sweep of suspected conspirators in Palmetto Bay, including Mr. Thornton's employers, and we've set up a command center at the sheriff's office. Miss Furay is there now—do you know where that is?"

"Yeah." I squinted in the sun, counted off seconds in my head, and hung up. I used my last quarter.

"I will have agents waiting to help you, Mr. Clay," the man went on as though I hadn't been chopping the conversation into little pieces. "You can meet them in the sheriff's office lobby." This time I hung up and walked back to the truck. I shared the orange juice and gum with Candy and pointed out the legal office. In less than a minute a small crowd of men in suits poured from the doors, and, in the second group, a bedraggled Katherine could be seen held tightly between two big men. She was still in the same white dress.

"Mom!" Candace shouted, and I grabbed her arm, holding her down until they drove away. "Let me go!" she screamed at me as the cars went through the traffic light and headed toward town.

"No!" I shouted back. "If they see you, they'll kill both of you and it's over! She's alive, Candy, she's alive! And, if we do the right things,

[123]

she'll stay that way." I let her go and she crossed her arms, leaning away from me. In her rage everyone was the enemy, including me.

Mark hadn't been in the group, and when I looked again, his was the only car still parked at the office. I pushed around a stack of soggy cards and papers that had been in my wallet and were now drying in the sunlight on the dash, found the right one, and held it out to Candace. She unwrapped a hand and took the card, looking down at it with disdain. "Can you drive this truck?" I asked, and she said she could.

"Good. I want you to drive through that intersection," I pointed, "and go north to the interstate. Don't stop until you get there. You'll see a Holiday Inn and you can call this number from there. Ask for Lieutenant Patrick, Candace, and tell him who you are. He'll come for you, and he'll bring help." She held the card in both hands as I slipped my pistol from the pouch and tucked it into my pants.

"What about you?" she said.

"I'm going to find out where Katherine is really going. I'll do everything I can to keep her safe, so hurry. Tell Patrick what really happened at Mel and Torrea's." I got out again, and Candy climbed over the shifter and settled into the driver's seat. She cranked the truck and reached out, squeezed my hand.

She put it in gear and I leaned against a car, watching until she was out of sight. I walked across the road to the office, crossed its small parking area, and stepped through the unlocked door into a cool, plant-filled interior. Mark was throwing papers into a briefcase, his coat hanging over the back of a chair. He looked up when I came in, and a handful of papers slid to the floor.

"Mac," he said, frozen as I crossed the room. A radio played low and, from the other room, a copier shuffled papers, throwing light against the wall as its top slipped back and forth.

"Hey, dickhead," I said. "You picked the wrong side."

SIXTEEN

I'm not a physical person, and even if I do wind up in a confrontation, I'm more of a counterpuncher. This was different, though, and as soon as I was in range I brought my fist up from my waist with an uppercut that slammed his gaping mouth shut. I hit him again with the same hand and finally whipped it around to the side of his face. I kept my left tucked close and out of the way. When he spun away, his feet tangled together and he crashed down onto the desktop, his elbows scattering pens and little framed pictures. I stepped closer and hit him three times in the kidney, punching as hard as I could, then grabbed his shirt and pulled him back until he fell to the floor. My knee came down hard on his sternum, and I dug my fingertips into his larynx and squeezed.

"Tell me everything, or I'll rip your fucking throat out." The venom in my words wasn't an act; I had to work to keep from crushing his windpipe with my fingers.

"Mac?" It came out as a coarse whisper. "Please."

"Where did they go?" I said through clenched teeth.

"The Sunset Hotel," Mark rasped. He raised a hand and put it on my wrist.

"Why do they want me to go to the sheriff's office?" He gripped my wrist weakly. His face was turning red. My eyes blurred and I couldn't catch my breath. I knew I was killing him, the man who sat up with me through months of booze and drugs, poured coffee, brought doughnuts, and kept me company after Sheevers died. My friend. I released his throat and sat back on my heels as he wheezed and searched for air. Fighter pilots in Vietnam had a saying: "You build a thousand bridges and you're a hero. But just let one of those bridges fall down on market day, and you're a bum again." Mark had lost a bridge.

"A trap," he said at last. "I was going there with these papers." He

[125]

waved toward his briefcase. "I thought maybe I could stop them. They're crazy, Mac. Out of control. They were going to kill both of you as soon as you got out of your car and say you flipped out—started shooting at them, you know? I just heard them say that as they went out the door." I stood up and turned my back on him, dug an assortment of pills from my shirt pocket, and walked to the water cooler. I swallowed the pills and took a long drink of cold water as Mark sat up. He leaned back against the front of his desk and rubbed his throat.

"Why did you do it, damn it!" I shouted. I spun around and threw the crushed paper cup at him.

"I was afraid," Mark said as he sat there, legs out, hands at his sides. "A soldier said he'd cut my throat, and I told him everything."

I got mad all over again. "They killed Mel and they're going to kill Katherine, you bastard!" I charged him and kicked the polished veneer beside his head. He didn't move. "What the fuck have you done?"

Mark stood up so fast he knocked his desk sideways. He stumbled toward me, face red and blue eyes blazing. "Goddamn you!" He shouted at me in a voice filled with rage. He was shaking. "Don't you ever talk to me like that again, you motherfucker!

"You never take responsibility for a fucking thing! Do you really want to know why Katherine is with those bastards?" He was crying. "Well, if you can't tell me, I can tell you. It's because you thought you could go up against the whole fucking world again, Mac. Your goddamned ego makes you think you're Zorro, or Superman. But you're not. You got Patty killed with your stupid games, and now Katherine and her daughter are in trouble.

"I know why I told them, Mac," he sniffed, and leaned back until he was staring at the ceiling fan. "I got scared of dying. I guess we're not all cut out for this kind of shit, buddy. But don't ever hit me again, or I'll have you thrown in jail." Mark walked to the cooler and took a drink. I leaned over the desk and lifted papers from his briefcase, looking at them as he composed himself. My emotions were yo-yoing, and I needed to find some control. Mark turned toward me, his face bruised and swollen.

"You know," he said, "there is never a day when I don't think about her. And I know that if it weren't for you, she'd still be here. She'd still be with me."

I felt old. Mark was right. I killed Patty, but her being with me had been Patty's choice, not his. And somewhere, the blame had to fall on those men whose power made them believe they didn't have to answer to anyone.

I spread the papers out on the desktop and looked them over. There were documents typed on Mark's letterhead that implicated the Men's Club and its members in a plot to subvert the Constitution of the United States, the current legal system, and the people of Florida. He had spent a great deal of time on them and they were very well written. There was a copy of the letter the speaker told the crowd about that night as I hid under the table. It was an incredible document. In paragraphs crammed with patriotic jargon, each member was guaranteed a small percentage of stock in the companies that were being formed to sell drugs in the state, and a chance to buy into a system that would privately finance these armies.

There was a Reagan administration study from the mid-eighties that explored the possibility of using private enterprise, borrowing huge sums of money through the banks and savings-and-loans, to purchase major military hardware like tanks and planes and battleships, then lease them to the services in a joint business venture. I heard Mark go into the other room, and when he came back to the desk, he had an armload of copies that he dropped on the blotter.

"I was going to take these to the authorities," he said. "I made up enough for the press and anyone else that might come to mind.

"I'm sorry, Mac," he said, "I thought I would be tougher than that, but I wasn't. There's no way to change it, but I really am sorry." I didn't want to talk about it any more. There were too many things still undone.

"Where did you get these?" I asked.

"Misters Barret, Barret and Finch are all on the board of directors at the Men's Club. I didn't think anything of it until you and I had that talk in the shopping center. They must've been the ones who told Birk about Katherine's trip to Tallahassee." Mark bent over the cooler again and drank more water.

"I broke into Finch's office last night, but they don't know it yet." He looked at me. "I hope you save her. Is her daughter dead?"

"No." I dug through the papers until I had one copy of each. I folded them and put them in my back pocket. "Give me your keys." Mark hesitated, but only for a second. He removed the car keys from a ring and handed them to me.

"If you call them and tell them I'm coming, Mark, you'll find out I'm more of a danger to you than they'll ever be. Do you understand?"

"Yes," he said. "But don't worry, I'm not going to do that. I really was going down there to try to stop them. I'll get these papers to a

[127]

friend of mine. He'll help me get them passed around." I headed for the door.

"Mac!" I looked at Mark over my throbbing shoulder. "They have over a thousand troops camped at Omni right now. I think they'll use them against you if they feel threatened, and you've really fucked things up for them."

"I hope they do," I said. "Maybe people will wake up when they see tanks in the streets." The sun seemed hotter and was a blinding white as I stepped outside. Mark's car cranked easily and the cool, conditioned air felt good on my face. Everything seemed crazy and unreal. I drove cautiously across the eastbound bridge that spanned Palmetto Bay, linking the beaches to the urban sprawl. The westbound bridge was clogged with tourists eager to get to their motel rooms, and traffic was backed up through three intersections. I took side roads and was downtown in less than ten minutes.

The business district had been built around the Sunset Hotel, and it dominated the skyline. Tall and wide and ancient, its facade was ominous, its presence imposing. Every important man who visited Palmetto Bay had stayed at least once at the Sunset. Photographs on the walls, some cracked and yellowed with age, showed politicians, dignitaries, and celebrities at the bar.

I had studied the Sunset Hotel with an intensity that I seldom achieved, Sheevers lying naked on my back as I propped myself up on my elbows, tangled in sheets and comforter. As I flipped the floor plans from page to page she leaned over my neck, whispered in my ear, and drew obscene stick fingers in every room. If they hadn't made any drastic changes in the layout, I knew I could find my way in and out of there in a hurry.

There was an ingenious system of stairs and narrow halls in the rear of the building designed to bring food and liquor, girls, boys, men, or women to the guests. I backed the Mercedes into a spot between two pickup trucks, and, with the darkly tinted windows up, I scanned my mind for the patterns of flow, the lengths of the hallways, and the angles of the stairs. I thought of them as tunnels and set myself to respond to them that way. I put my senses on alert and hoped I hadn't lost too much over the years.

Mark's fedora lay on the passenger seat, and I put it on before I got out, kept my head down, and crossed the alley quickly. Once inside the service door, I tossed the hat into a trash barrel and pulled the pistol from my belt. I strained to hear the sounds of the building, and soon an aura of noise surrounded me, lifted me up the stairs past tall,

[128]

wooden doors with ornate knobs and, high above, stained-glass transoms. I could hear conversations and feel the movement of air against my cheeks, could feel the vibrations of the hotel through my fingertips and smell perfumes, cigars, and food.

My feet moved surely on the carpeted stairs and swiftly down the halls. People stirred in some rooms; other rooms were silent. It was a little after one o'clock in the afternoon, and there was no activity in this part of the Sunset; too late for lunch, too early for sex. I struggled to maintain my sensory discipline, and was exhausted by the time I had finished the second floor. When I reached the third I thought that maybe I was just wishing it, but I heard a voice familiar to me and smelled Katherine's faint perfume. I put my fingers on the walls and traced my way to the fourth door. There, just a few feet away from me, was Katherine Furay. I knew it.

I heard two men talking low, then recoiled at the abrasive voice of Tommy Lovett. He was saying nasty things about me and laughing. I did not hear Katherine, and I wondered if she might be dead. At that point it didn't matter. I was going in. I shifted the pistol to my slow left hand and aimed it at the lock, just in case. With the right I twisted the knob and found it unlocked, pushed open the door, and raised the pistol as I stepped inside. Two silver-haired men in expensive suits sat in overstuffed chairs and Tommy Lovett leaned on the wall between them, his arms folded across his chest. Startled, they almost bolted, but I swung the pistol in a slow curve that covered them and said, "Don't."

"Mac!" Katherine leapt to her feet from a daybed along the wall and stopped short of embracing me.

"Hey, Bubba," I said to her, and turned slightly, moving the heavy pistol back into my right hand. The left hand already started icing up and going numb. "Candace is alive and safe."

"Oh," she inhaled the word, "thank God!"

"Mr. Clay," one of the men said. I motioned to Katherine and she stepped behind me, between the gun and the door.

"Yeah?" I cocked my head toward him but kept my eyes on Tommy Lovett.

"It seems we've underestimated you more than once," he said. Lovett snorted.

"Thanks for the compliment," I said. "But I think it's more likely you're just been overestimating yourselves." I felt Katherine's fingers caress my back. A door closed down the hall, and I heard men's voices coming closer.

[129]

Katherine slammed the door shut and turned the deadbolt, and someone began yelling and pounding. Lovett eased away from the wall and the men gripped the arms of their chairs. I raised the pistol to Lovett's head and told him to stop. He did. "Tell them to back off," I said to the younger silver-haired man, and he shouted to get their attention.

"Don't come in," he said to the door. "Stay where you are. We're having a bit of a problem."

"Good," I said. "Let's keep cool." I thought of Candace and Lonnie Patrick and wondered how he would find us, wished I'd thought about stuff like this ahead of time.

"It seems obvious that you're not going anywhere." The same man continued. The other, softer and older with limpid eyes and bony fingers, sat like a stone. Tommy, a small, wiry ferret with darting eyes, would have looked more natural in a dress than in the ridiculous silk suit he wore. I watched the other two and saw how tightly their skin was stretched across their faces, lips twisted in thin grimaces, neck veins bulging. These guys were stressed out, power junkies with a shortage of junk. I realized that, even it they got rid of the bunch of us now and destroyed all the evidence, Bob Birk's campaign was tainted. And they had already hitched their wagon to his rising star.

We had won, sort of. If not a victory, we had at least put a spotlight on these cockroaches of the game, the boys who like doing it in the dark. Each plan for a new Florida would have to be reconsidered, and, who knows, maybe some reporter would not only stumble over the story but have a boss who'd print it. They were remote chances, but these were people who didn't take chances. I felt a little better. "Boy," I said, "you guys really botched this thing, didn't you?"

"I'm sure you believe that what you're doing is right." The talker's eyes were burning with rage. I had humiliated him. "But you just don't understand what's at stake here. We'll find Miss Furay's daughter and take whatever steps necessary to correct the damage you've done. It's an inconvenience, but it's just another lesson we must learn. Loose ends, Mr. Clay, can be very costly." He practically cooed at me from the chair.

"You're a dinosaur and you know it," he continued, "one of those useless and unnecessary creatures that doesn't know when to quit. Under normal circumstances, I would have sympathy for someone like you.

"But you're hurting America's future, and I can't excuse it. We've been living a lie." He smiled, and I let my eyes drift past him a little,

[130]

watching for any movement from the other two. The men in the hallway were silent. The front door to the room was closed, and Katherine slipped over and locked it too, then returned to me.

"We want the problems to solve themselves, but they won't." The guy was warming up. "Drugs are ruining us, destroying the economy and the will of the people. Indecision is killing our politicians, and, thank God, we have a few real men left who will act to make things right again.

"The people of Florida will be proud of themselves when they see what they've done. When they see how much safer their streets are, how much nicer their neighborhoods and towns will be when we put dope addicts and disgruntled dissidents like you in places where they don't have to worry about you."

So, I thought, *they're planning on arresting a few thousand subversives and dangerous politicians along the way?* That made sense.

"Property values will rise, decent people will move here, and, with the services people like you will provide, living expenses and taxes will go down." His smile became a smirk. "Now do you see the future, Mr. Clay?" I kept staring at the wall.

"Mr. Clay?" he repeated himself. I blinked rapidly and let my eyes focus on his face.

"I'm sorry," I said. "Were you talking at me?"

Katherine laughed and the man glared at me, his fatherly act gone. "I never should have expected you to grasp the complexities of our goals."

·"Oh," I said, "I have no problem with the politics or sociology, I'm just not that interested in those things right now. You see, I'm trying to find a gang of psychopaths who murdered four people at Limestone Creek about five years ago. Two of the victims were children."

"Don't be absurd!" he said. "Those weren't children, they were drug sellers, dope addicts!"

"Yeah," I said, "and Mel Shiver was a dealer too. Shut up, old man." I was bored with this drivel, and it was keeping my mind away from solving the minor problem of getting out alive. I heard a commotion in the front room, and someone rattled the knob on that door too. Things were getting a little tight.

Katherine edged around until she was at my side again. She reached carefully forward and pulled a folded paper from a small table beside the older man, uncovering a small pistol hidden beneath it. I hadn't noticed it.

"Leave it alone, bitch!" Tommy Lovett snapped at her, his eyes

[131]

following her hand as she picked up the gun. It was a .25 automatic. The old guy had been slowly leaning in its direction, and now he slumped back in the chair.

"Thanks, pal," I said.

"Don't mention it." Her voice was a wonderful thing. Tommy Lovett shifted positions, and I watched him closely. He stretched his lips into a cold smile.

"I hate to see you die before we get your little girl," he said to Katherine. "She was a hot little piece of ass, and I was hoping you'd be there to see what I do to her.

"I think I'll chop her up like I done his old girlfriend." He looked at me, and my world was reduced to an area no larger than Tommy Lovett. I felt a bitter heat spread through my stomach and into my chest.

"Lovett," the other man said. "Stop."

Tommy stared into my eyes. "You should've heard the noises she made every time I stabbed her, Clay," he said. "It was like I was fuckin' her."

The fire raced down my arm and into my hand, into the finger coiled around the trigger. My head felt as though it was going to explode, but the rage rendered me immobile, and in that instant, they reacted. So did I, but it was a second too late. The silver-haired talker grabbed a glass ashtray and tossed it like a Frisbee at my face. I ducked it and came around, getting a shot off in his direction, but even as I did, I saw Lovett move around the chair. He grabbed a heavy brass floor lamp and swung it like a baseball bat. The solid base smashed into my left shoulder and ruptured the healing wound, ripping into the swollen flesh under my makeshift bandage.

I couldn't move, couldn't even think because of the pain. He brought the lamp back and reloaded to swing again, stepping into it this time like a major leaguer, but I heard two loud pops and his silk suit erupted in twin fountains of blood. He slammed back into the wall.

"Bastard!" Katherine shouted as she shot him a third time, and the sound was buried in the noises made by both doors being bashed in. The old guy stayed in the chair, and as I gripped my shoulder and dropped to my knees, I saw the talker slumped in the corner of the room with an ugly red hole in his neck. Katherine stood over me as people poured into the room from both sides.

SEVENTEEN

There was a whole lot of shooting going on, and I wasn't doing any of it. I saw Lonnie Patrick and four other men burst through the front door, weapons up, just a moment before the back door caved in, and in a wall-splintering hail of fire, one of his men grabbed his side and stumbled. Lonnie and the other three stood their ground, and in less than five seconds, it was over.

Katherine was trying to pull me to my feet, and Patrick joined her, dropping under my bloody shoulder and lifting me until I was attached to his side, my own pistol hanging uselessly in my other hand. People were yelling and running up the back stairs, and with the lieutenant shouting orders, we raced out the front door, down a large stairwell filled with frightened people, and into a lobby filled with guns.

I say "we" raced. Actually, I was a floppy puppet, dangling from Lonnie Patrick with the tips of my shoes scooting across the green wool carpet, leaving wobbly trails in the thick nap. Men came through the beveled-glass entry doors on the run, shooting at us. I saw them drop as the doors disintegrated. We made it to the steps and into the street before the next group challenged us, and they were overpowered by Lonnie's tiny army.

I felt my right leg flop out and back in like rubber, and I knew I'd been shot in the thigh. Lonnie tossed me into the back seat of a large van and Katherine fell in beside me, saying things I couldn't understand as she put her arms around me. My head drooped onto her soft chest and I couldn't raise it.

With everyone inside, Lonnie gunned the engine and we swung into the street, bumped a couple of cars, and picked up speed. He shouted over his shoulder at me as my head lolled dumbly against the woman I loved. "Cole Younger was shot twenty-six times and he lived to be an old man!" he said. "Hang on, Clay. You can do it!"

I'm sure that was supposed to reassure me, but it didn't. He checked with everyone else in the van, and two other had been hit at least once. In their bulletproof Mylar vests they'd formed a shield around Katherine, and she was unhurt. I heard the engine winding up under the load and we bounced through a few intersections, slid into a couple of turns, and surged forward as the distant sound of a siren sawed its way into the open windows.

"Damn it!" Patrick cursed and slapped the steering wheel. "I'm not shooting at cops. I don't care—I can't shoot a cop!" The others murmured agreement, and we picked up more speed but were no match for the sheriff's deputy, his siren closer and louder, grating on my nerves until he pulled alongside and, over the scream of his siren, a voice bellowed from the car's external speaker.

"Foller May!" the deputy shouted. "Foller May!"

"What the hell's he saying?" Patrick screamed at anyone and everyone. I recognized the voice and pulled myself up far enough to look out the window.

"That's Willis!" I said to Patrick. "Willis Traxler! He's saying, 'Follow me!' Do it!"

The patrol car whipped in front of the van and Willis escorted us away from town. I tried to pay attention, but Katherine was so soft and her hands were so comforting that I kept falling asleep. It seemed a silly thing to do under the circumstances, but I couldn't help it. As I got sleepier I also got lighter, until I floated right out of her arms and spread myself out along the underside of the car's headliner, looking down curiously at a van full of rumpled people, a beautiful woman deep in the back seat hanging on to an empty rag doll. I could see the speedometer in front of the driver, and its needle was pegged at ninety-five. Everything was so peaceful that I decided to slip out the window and soar away, but at that moment, Patrick braked violently, leaned hard to the right, and left the paved road. The van clattered over a railroad crossing and came down hard on a bumpy clay road. I slammed back into my body and my teeth rattled together painfully. My shoulder had gone from a real thing to a piece of abstract art that could have been titled "Jell-O, With Knives."

"Don't die," Katherine whispered in my ear. "I love you."

I got serious and tried to return the words, but they came out, "Foo doo." I didn't try again.

Dust billowed in through the van windows as we raced for miles over winding dirt and clay roads that sometimes deteriorated into bumpy double-rutted pig trails, packed with holes that jarred the van's frame and gnawed at the tailpipe. Lost in the cloud of dust roiling up

[134]

behind Willis in the hot, still air, Patrick kept braking hard at sudden sharp turns banked with thick sand. My limp body knocked against Katherine, and each time our wheels caught in the sand she held me, kept me from tumbling into the floor.

Willis never slowed down. Driving over untended dirt trails he'd grown up on, he treated his patrol car like a pulpwood truck, drawing us along behind. In the dust was the smell of pine, the sweet scent of wild berries, and the feel of freedom. It seemed we'd never stop, but at last I felt the van clatter across the long wooden bridge to Willis Traxler's family homestead.

Hunting dogs hooted from their pens and yard dogs barked joyfully. People called out, and I heard Willis shouting instructions from his car window even as we tore into the dirt yard that I knew well. There were three large clapboard-frame houses under a stand of giant oaks, facing a sandy yard with ragged islands of grass. Four mobile homes sat here and there behind the houses, and everywhere the bones of defeated machinery lay picked over by skilled hands. Ancient cars and old trucks lined a dark cypress slough filled with lily pads and black water. Even as I lay against Katherine with my eyes closed, I could see this warm and friendly place, could hear the Traxler women hurrying to the van. Willis ran from window to window and diagnosed the wounds, helped us out to where the women could judge our needs.

This was a large family, and they had been living and dying on the same piece of land for well over a hundred years. A part of that large sea of Americans with no health insurance and no retirement, they had it better than many. Pulpwooding is a dangerous job and physically demanding. The system for treating an injured man had been developed and finely tuned by generations of Traxler women.

The men wouldn't be home before eight o'clcock, but there was a sufficient army to help us into the main house. Willis's house. Hands grappled with me and I was raised in the air, then carried inside and lowered onto a mattress. My clothes were ripped from me and someone pushed me around. I smelled disinfectant and felt dull thumps on my shoulder and leg. I wanted to get up and participate, but it was like being filled with feathers and stones. The afternoon sunlight sliced in through long windows, and dust sparkled and danced upward in the beams. People moved around me and talked in low voices. They slid me to the middle of the bed and Katherine put her palm on my cheek. I couldn't talk.

Lonnie Patrick's face hovered over mine, and he grinned. "This woman must be brain-damaged," he said, and I heard Katherine tell him to leave me alone.

[135]

"He'll live," somebody said, then added, "I think."

Willis leaned down and patted my face with a beefy hand. "You're on my bed, Mackey boy. A lot of lives was started right there, so don't you mess it up by dyin' on it." His hand was gentle. He straightened up, laughed, and I saw him put his arm around Katherine as though he'd known her forever. He led her away, and from somewhere outside I could hear children playing. Someone pulled a string, and the overhead light went off. The curtains were pulled together and I was left alone.

We had tried hard, but, in the end, it comes down to whether you did it or you didn't do it. And the job was still undone. Birk still made his way toward the statehouse and the general and his troops still waited to be unleashed. I worried over this as I watched the changing patterns of shadow and light that filtered through the curtains and painted the tongue-and-groove ceiling with fantastic shapes, reflections of anything the imagination chose to make them. The door opened, and I smelled food cooking.

Katherine held my good hand, and I tried to remember something important. Something I wanted to say. I heard the bed squeak, felt it shift as she sat beside me.

"Pocket," I said.

"What?" She leaned down.

"Pocket." The one word was exhausting. She looked in my eyes and spoke the word again, as a question.

"Pocket," I whispered, and waited. Katherine stood up and turned in a circle, searching. She walked away and returned with my bloody clothes. She glanced at me, and I tried to nod. Her fingers dug through the shirt, emptied my pants pockets, and held up the folded pages.

"This," she said.

"Yes," I said. She sat down and switched on the bedside lamp. A golden light from its shade painted her sad face.

"Candy?" I forced the word "Okay?" Her features relaxed a little.

"Yes, thanks to you. Lonnie sent her to Tallahassee with his family," Katherine said, turning the paper over in her hands as she looked in my eyes. "Then he came to Palmetto Bay in the van with the other men." She opened the pages I had taken from Mark's office and read, looking up once.

"Mark stayed in his office until Lonnie came, Mac," she said. "He told him where we were."

"Good," I said. "Good for him." She read more, going through the pages as I watched her eyes. I saw the disbelief, the anger.

"Show Patrick," I said. I stretched my back and worked at moving

[136]

my good arm and leg while she was gone. When she returned, Lonnie was with her. They carried soup and medicine.

"Incredible!" Lonnie said, holding up the pages. "Where'd you get these?" I told him, and he nodded. "That guy's beating himself to death over this."

"I know." I glanced at Katherine and wondered if we all looked that haggard. "He just got scared."

"Mac," Patrick said, "I'm taking these with me to Tallahassee. I'd say we're in a hell of a lot of trouble right now, but I'm glad we could help. I've shown the tapes around discreetly, and I think we'll have some support when we get home. These papers will help me explain to my chief why I did a John Wayne thing here today.

"I have to tell you, sport," he coughed, "we're outmanned and outgunned, but I think they know we're here now.

"I need to get two of my men to the hospital, soon. They'll be okay," he said. "These ladies did a great job on them. Your pal Willis is a wild man."

"I know," I said. "Thanks for getting us out."

He nodded at me, winked at Katherine. "I can't believe you have a full-grown daughter. If I wasn't happily married and twice as old as Candy," he said, "I would overwhelm her."

Katherine laughed. "I've never heard it put quite that way, Lieutenant, but I'd bet you could do it."

Lonnie stepped out of the room and came back with the other four men, two in bandages. He introduced them to us and said, "We made waves today and I'm not sure what they're going to do to us when we get back, but we know why we did it and it's going to be okay. They can't hide this anymore, and that makes me feel damned good." He glanced at Katherine. "I'll get Candace back to you as soon as I can." It was an awkward moment, and none of us knew how to get out of it.

The radio in the kitchen was tuned to a local station, and the music was interrupted every ten minutes or so by live reports from downtown Palmetto Bay. Stunned reporters told fantastic tales, stumbling over conflicts between the official story and eyewitness reports. But, by any account, it was carnage.

Four dead, officially, and over ten others in the hospital. One confused newsman tried to combine the official "mob-style hit" story with accounts that it was really cops staging a daring rescue at the Sunset Hotel. He gave up and signed off. Sheriff Hall vowed to catch the "drug kingpins" who killed Tommy Lovett in cold blood. By four o'clock, the special bulletins had become a boring drone.

[137]

The Tallahassee cops had made phone calls home and were clearly anxious to leave, but Willis held them there until he could arrange for safe transportation back. The van was hidden from sight by Willis and Lonnie, covered and stored until this thing could be settled. As we sat waiting, we discussed the situation.

After the news at four, the familiar theme song of Red Flannery's "Talk-to-Me-America Show" started playing, and it seemed out of place in the tense house. "Ladies and gentlemen," Red's resonant voice took over. "I have a very different show for you today and I ask you to call your friends and neighbors, call your relatives and ask them to listen, because their lives are in danger. Some of you have been with me for twenty years, and, I'll tell you now, this may be our last day together. Because I'm going to keep telling this story until something is done about it, or until I'm removed from the air. So stay with me." Even in our impossible situation I noticed the others lean toward the open door, toward the sound of Red Flannery.

"My best friend died yesterday, and his death is on my shoulders," he said. "You see, he came to me for help and I denied him. I'm a busy man, a celebrity.

"My dearest friend." His voice was masterfully deep and sincere. "I've know him for almost thirty years, but when he came to Mobile a couple of days ago, I refused to see him. He had sent me a fantastic story a couple of weeks back and, truthfully, I thought he'd gone over the edge. When he came to Mobile he brought a box full of things, but we never talked. He had stumbled over a wild plot and was afraid that someone had discovered him, that his life was in danger. That's what he told my secretary. But I'm a busy man, a celebrity. Heard from Key West to Alaska.

"I told my secretary to be polite but send him away." His voice faltered. "My friend's name was Mel Shiver, and he was murdered yesterday by men disguised as DEA agents, killed by evil men for the crime of patriotism.

"Please stay with me and let me tell you his story," Red Flannery said. The distant sounds of laughing children were the only sounds in the universe. Flannery spun his web in a brilliant blend of theater and factual reporting as we listened, spellbound. Even without all the facts, he wove together audio cuts from the videotapes, Mel's research, and his own skillful style into a powerful, cohesive sequence of events that told the story of politics, corruption, and death.

An oven door was opened, then closed. "Lord have mercy," a woman said from the kitchen.

[138]

EIGHTEEN

I threw down my crutches and walked carefully but triumphantly from the porch into the gray dirt yard, raised my arms, and looked into the cloudy sky. "Praise Jesus!" I shouted. "I'm healed!"

"Don't mock the Lord," Mae Traxler said from her rocker, never looking up from a basket of butter beans.

"Yes, ma'am," I mumbled. Katherine and her pretty daughter watched from the shade as I exercised in the yard. Each day seemed a little better than the one before, and I was getting control back in my left hand.

Each sunrise was a little hotter, and the humidity stayed near one hundred percent. Sometimes it rained late at night and the air turned cooler as we lay together talking. Candace spent her nights one room away, and when she couldn't sleep Katherine would go to her. The Traxler family adjusted to our presence the same way they adjusted to everything. Extra dishes were set out at mealtime and the kids doubled up in their beds. No explanations were required.

I watched Katherine's dark eyes as they followed my brief workout. She, too, was trying to heal. A few weeks earlier, we had spent a long night worrying over an infection in my shoulder before Mae Traxler's remedies began to work, and, sometime before dawn, Candace started telling her mother the story of her time with Lovett's Sunset girls.

"God," she'd said, pacing at the foot of the bed. "It was another person who did those things. I mean, it didn't even matter to me what anyone wanted. I didn't care. Just as long as they gave me some money to hang out with." She made her way to Katherine, and they embraced.

"I'm sorry," she said. "I tried to tell you once, after Bob Birk raped me. He was crazy, Mom. He shot at one girl, and he broke Janice's arm. I saw him do it. He told everybody he was Rambo.

"It was horrible, but in a way I needed that to come to my senses." She broke away from Katherine.

"I never went back." Candy looked at me. "I came to your house one time," she said. "You weren't there, but Aunt Patty was, and I told her everything—but I made her swear she wouldn't tell."

"She didn't say anything to me about it," I said, remembering how much Patty hated the crowd downtown.

"I always thought she died because of me," Candy said. A rooster began to crow outside, and gray light began seeping through the closed curtains.

"No," I said. "You had nothing to do with it."

We sent handwritten transcripts and tape recordings to Mr. Robert Booth Holmes, the Tallahassee lawyer who changed my mind about lawyers. He seemed to be everywhere at once. He'd filed lawsuits against everyone from the President to the hotel bellboy, worked with the police-union lawyers, and blocked attempts to jail Lonnie Patrick and the other four officers. He even negotiated benefits for them during their suspensions.

Willis Traxler lied through his teeth. He shuffled and spit and told the sheriff how he'd chased us to the county line and danged near wrecked his patrol car chasing us down every dirt road in the Panhandle before he lost us. After being reprimanded for not calling for backup, ignoring procedure, he was back on the job. No one in Palmetto Bay knew where we were. The three of us had vanished, and we hoped to keep it that way.

Each day I got stronger, and with the strength came more anger. Where there should have been the satisfaction of knowing Katherine and her daughter were safe there was only an empty feeling, a cold knowledge that the danger was still there. Red Flannery was still on the air, but his story was going up in smoke. The four house bills were quietly removed from consideration by the legislature. The phantom army vanished, and as the gubernatorial primary loomed just around the corner, Bob Birk was kissing hands and shaking babies in a virtual assembly line across the Sunshine State. Those who decide what's news and what isn't buried the shoot-out at the Sunset Hotel in the back pages, obscured the lawsuits, and ignored Red Flannery. Even desperate, they were incredible. The legal battle raged on backstage.

Flannery's suggestion to "just say no" to all pollsters seemed to be having an effect on the political coverage. He'd begun a campaign of his own, saying no matter what your politics or your party, if everyone refused to answer pollsters' questions the politicians would be forced to commit themselves to a platform. There were reports that polling accuracy had dropped. Still, Birk seemed to be holding a sizable lead in popularity among those who answered. Time seemed suspended.

I woke up after midnight on primary morning and saw Katherine standing at the window, her arms crossed, head leaning against the frame. "What's on your mind?" I said. She didn't move, and after a long while I decided she didn't want to talk. I lay back and closed my eyes. When she came back to bed, Katherine stretched out beside me and draped an arm across my stomach, her head on my shoulder.

"I killed someone," she said. "And I can't get it out of my mind. . . . I mean, I know why I did it and I'd do it again, but, Mac, I killed a man." I rubbed her neck softly and kept quiet as she talked. An hour passed as she told me about her family, how her mother had died just months after her father. Her voice was like a slow stream, and the story of her childhood flowed into the birth of Candy and of being a mother at fifteen. She talked about taking a bus to Las Vegas, of looking for work and trying to protect her daughter. Somewhere in the conversation she fell asleep, and I lay motionless in the dark feeling her heart tapping against me, and I wanted to be twenty feet tall and mean as hell. I wanted to guarantee her no harm would ever come to her again, and I cursed myself because it was beyond my power. Her breathing was deep and even, and she was relaxed in her sleep.

"I love you," I said.

I was sitting in a chair on the front porch when Lonnie Patrick drove up in a battered old Chevrolet. The dogs barked until I stood up and leaned on the railing, then they slipped gratefully back into the cool sand under the house. Even at dawn the heat was like a heavy blanket. A dense gray fog hung an inch above the water, and black cypress stumps stuck their heads out of the top. Beyond them a peach-colored line divided the earth from the sky.

I had been awake early, sharing coffee with Mother Mae as the other Traxler women prepared their day's supplies, jugs of water, and slices of pie. They laughed and talked among themselves as I sat with Mae in her kitchen, a place that always smelled like tomatoes and cigarette smoke.

Katherine and Candace had been working in the fields with them for days, but we'd received word from Lonnie that he had something to tell us and that he would arrive early, so they slept in.

"We'll be finished with the peas by noon today." Mae spoke around a Pall Mall cigarette, its ash long and unstable. "And we'll start canning tonight. Willis and Addie and the kids are doing just fine over there, so don't you worry about that. The three of you can come over this evenin' and we'll make a night of it." The ash fell to the bare tabletop and she brushed it over the side.

"I'm scared for Willis, Mac. He thinks everything's a game."

"I'll talk to him, but I think he knows what he's doing, Mae," I said as they carried everything to the "yard truck," a flatbed truck that may have once had a brand name, a body style. There were no fenders, and they had kept the body hammered into a trucklike shape. It had one headlight and one taillight, and the crumpled tag was over twenty years old. This was the work machine, and it never left Traxler land. The women would have its flatbed stacked high with hampers of peas when they returned. They had been in the fields for almost an hour when Lonnie showed up.

"Hey, hero," he said as he climbed from the sedan.

"Fuck off." I made my way down the steps.

"Where is everybody?" he said.

"Katherine's asleep," I said. "So is Candy. The others are picking peas. What's the story?"

"Well . . ." He pulled a briefcase through the open window and used the hood for a table, shuffling papers together before he removed them. He waved them at me and smiled. "I've had people working overtime in the archives, in the document files in Tallahassee. They found these." He handed them to me, and I leafed through them.

They were photocopies of contracts between government officials and the board of Omni, signed documents authorizing percentages of profit to Omni members in exchange for the chance to develop a new type of army on the Omni grounds. A Top Secret stamp marked each page, but I didn't care how he'd obtained them. Bob Birk's name was at the top of each line of signatures. The date on each page was June the twelfth, the same as the wild party at the Sunset Hotel and the rape of Candace Furay.

"Holy cow," I said.

"Wait until you see the one from the FDLE," Lonnie said, and pulled out a stapled folder with the Florida Department of Law Enforcement letterhead. He'd obviously been getting a lot of help from high places. "They're investigating your sheriff in connection with the Limestone Creek Murders and the death of the black dope pusher."

"Good morning, handsome," Katherine called out from the porch, and we both turned toward the house. She looked at me and wrinkled her face. "Not you, sweetie." Candy opened the screen door and peeked out.

"Come inside," Katherine said, "and show me what you have."

"How could I resist an invitation like that?" Lonnie said, taking the papers from me and stuffing them back into the briefcase. He snapped it closed and straightened up. "Out of my way, crip." He pushed me aside and headed for the porch. "You can catch up to us later."

They all went inside, but I lingered, sweat trickling under my bandages as I stood beside the car. I thought of the documents, the other paperwork, and the women who were still willing to testify against Birk if we ever made it to trial. For the very first time since Katherine knocked on my door, I mulled over the possibility of success. We had a case for murder at Omni.

A big fish broke the water somewhere in the fog, and I heard him swirl quickly before he was gone. Willis and I had fished these backwaters until I knew every inch of them, and I imagined a big bass rolling on the surface, swallowing a spider, a hapless cricket, a minnow. I remembered what I'd said to Lonnie Patrick as I gathered my clothes from the lawn that night, and wondered how the bass would react with a minnow lodged in its throat. It wouldn't just sink and die.

I walked to the muddy edge of the slough and circled to the right, past the junked timber trucks and the carefully tended bass boats, skirted a mountain of burned trash that rose from a deep pit, and sat on the tall, worn tire of an old tractor, my legs dangling over the side. I slapped the injured leg and it hurt, but not much. I tried rolling my shoulder, but it told me it wasn't ready for that.

I closed my eyes and added my new facts to the mental files. Somewhere, someone knew the soldier who murdered Candy's friends. When the story broke, there was a minor flurry of activity from their parents, but as the facts were twisted around and reburied, the broken families willingly returned to anonymity, back to their sad lives. I wanted them to have their day, to know what had really happened to their children. The family of Renaldo Tippit deserved no less.

I added and deleted, watched a hopeful pattern emerge. I wanted to go even deeper, but I heard the swirl of water again and this time it was no fish. I listened closer as I struggled back up to the real world, to my normal state of semiconciousness. I wondered how long I'd been sitting there. The noise came again. It was the sound of an oar being drawn carefully through the water. I opened my eyes and shook my head. The sun had risen well over a wall of cypress trees on the far side of the slough, and its blistering heat was cutting holes in the fog.

I squinted into the brightness, and off to my left, coming out of one of the narrow channels that gave access to the Traxler slough, was a long black boat. Sleek and dark, it floated out of the fog like a wraith, its presence evil enough even before I saw the lone man rise from behind the windshield. He was dressed in black and had dark grease paint smeared across his cheeks and forehead. He bent down and dropped the oar soundlessly into the boat, and when he came back up, there was a hand-held rocket launcher balanced on his shoulder; one of the Stinger-type missiles that our government traded like baseball cards to third-world countries.

My first thought was a dumb one. I thought he was going to blow up the tractor, but I don't think he even saw me. He turned casually until his little launcher was pointed just to the right of Lonnie's car, directly in line with the screen door that stood in the middle of the front porch. Before I could crawl down from the big tire I heard a swoosh, and the explosion threw me to the wet ground, the heat singeing the hairs on my arms.

I leapt to my feet and clawed my way around the trash pile, only to stand dumbly watching as the few charred remains of Willis Traxler's home folded in on themselves in a fiery roar. Behind me, the man cranked his engine and it puttered a few seconds before he opened the throttle and slipped back into the fog.

"No!" I shouted at him, running to the three boats tied to a small, rough-cut cypress dock. I looked back over my shoulder, but the remains of the house were just a small stack of burning black timbers. The windows of Lonnie's car were shattered, and, though the fire hadn't spread, the other houses had suffered from the blast. My heart was ice cold and my hands were rock steady as I untied the faster of the three boats, squeezed some gas through the line, and cranked the boat.

I don't think he was in a hurry until he heard me start up, but I heard his boat rev up, pictured it in my mind as it cut through the channel. I twisted the throttle and shot from the dock in pursuit, wondering at first why he wasn't outrunning me. In a boat like his, it should have been no contest. Then I realized he wasn't familiar with the series of channels cut in the dense cypress swamp and he was having to find his way between the unseen walls of submerged stumps. I listened to him and could tell by his changes in direction and speed where he would end up when he finally hit the river, and I opened the throttle the rest of the way, felt the wet air on my face push hot tears from my eyes. My lips were stretched tightly and pulled away from my teeth in a snarl, muscles so rigid that I felt the ones in my neck jumping.

This man's death was all I had to live for, and I put my entire self into the chase. The boat bucked and slapped over familiar waters, and I cut every corner, feeling the thump every time I drifted off course and touched one of the hidden trees. Long fingers of mist reached from the slough into the river, and I brought the bow of the boat up like a knife blade, cutting the mist into swirling pieces. I turned the boat down-river, toward the winding course the man in the black boat had taken, and I saw him slipping the boat's nose into the deep water just as I ripped through the last line of fog and bore down on him.

I didn't slow down. He raised an automatic rifle with a banana clip and almost got it pointed in my direction before I rammed his boat with mine. The metal hull screeched and shook, and everything in the boat flew into the air. I tried to hold on but couldn't. The throttle was torn from my grasp and I crashed into just about every part of the boat before it bobbed to a stop, intact.

I picked myself up, clutching my useless shoulder, and looked around. The black fiberglass boat had virtually exploded, and ragged chunks of things floated in the rippled water. The hull of my boat was twisted and bent, but I saw no leaks yet. The boat bobbed in a circle and I watched for the man, wishing I had a weapon. I didn't need one.

Nothing looks more useless and ugly than a dead human being. There's a perversity to what we leave behind: a soft, puffy and pitifully shaped piece of meat. This man was undeniably dead and I didn't want to touch him, but I wanted to know who sent him.

I reached down and grabbed his shirt, lost my grip, and tried again, gaining a new respect for Candace as I dragged the body on board. It seemed impossible that she could have found the strength to pull me up on that riverbank. Even thinking of Katherine and the others dead in the inferno of the Traxler home, I couldn't scrape up enough emotion to hate this empty thing. I felt my shield rising around me again, cutting off the new emotions I'd been savoring. I was as hollow a shell as this nameless body, and I began the mechanical process of trying to row the bent boat toward the land with one arm and one oar.

There was only one public boat landing for miles on this part of the river, and I headed for it. I hoped someone would be there to help me. There was no way I'd be able to swim to shore, and I wanted to survive. I hadn't searched the man's pockets yet, but I knew beyond a doubt that Bob Birk had sent him, whether or not it was endorsed by his handlers. This was personal. I didn't know how he found us, but I was going to find him. I vowed to myself that it would end before the day was out. Birk would be dead or I would die trying.

It took over an hour to row the boat to the secluded landing, and just as I turned into the entry channel, a couple of boats raced by at full speed. Someone had undoubtedly found the remains of this guy's craft.

There was a truck and empty trailer at the landing, but no people were in sight. I shouted a few times, then gave up, forced the boat onto the bank and climbed carefully over the side, waded to shore, and tugged it up a grassy bank.

The truck was locked and there were no houses in sight, so I sat down on the bank and rested. My leg wouldn't last much longer and the shoulder was already gone. I thought of Katherine again, but already she seemed distant to me. I had room for only one thing in my mind. Bob Birk occupied all the territory. There was nothing else. I waited but no one came, so I limped back to the boat and turned the man over. I searched his pockets, but there was no wallet and no change, just a half-eaten roll of Tums and a set of keys. He was already cold, and I removed them quickly. On a hunch, I went to the truck and tried the keys. One fit the door lock and I opened it, sat down inside and cranked it up, then climbed back out.

The boat trailer separated easily from the ball, and I pushed it away. I dug under the seat and found a Smith & Wesson .38-caliber revolver, loaded. A Remington thirty-caliber rifle with a scope was cradled in a rack above the seat. The pistol went in my belt. There was nothing in this world that could hold my attention. The landscape passed by unnoticed, the wind on my face wasn't soothing, and the life around me was without consequence. They wouldn't stop me from getting to Bob Birk, from taking his worthless life, but knowing that didn't mean anything to me. It was a job to be done. When I drove under the interstate it seemed strange that so many hundreds of people had nothing better to do with their time than to drive around aimlessly. Didn't they know there was a war going on?

[146]

NINETEEN

Glossy red, white, and blue rectangles were plastered on everything, and most seemed to have Birk's name on them. We'd heard on the radio that his staff had planned a large victory reception for him at his business office, a large brick building facing the bay on the front and an enclosed courtyard to the rear. His choice as the party candidate during this primary was a given.

Time was no big deal anymore either, so I stopped by the cemetery first, drove to Sheevers's grave, and said good-bye. So much had changed. I cruised around in the dead man's truck while I searched for a plan. I was in no shape to simply run in with guns blazing. The front of the office was alive with well-dressed men and women stringing colored foil ribbons and passing out literature to people on their way to the polls to vote. New cars were arriving as others pulled away, and everyone seemed so goddamned happy.

The general and his troops, one of them a man who murdered a fifteen-year-old girl in cold blood, had gone away, but not for good. Under Birk's command as governor, they would simply bide their time, wait for the right sequence of events, and it would be back on line again. I drove past the jubilant crowd, pulled around the block, and examined the two buildings on the back side of the block. The taller one was a state office building, filled with administrators and engineers. The other, less well kept, had once been a hotel, but the Sunset cut its own rates, ran a high-powered advertising campaign, and added a few amenities for a time, and this hotel's owners threw in the towel. A triumphant Sunset Hotel board of directors bought the building and turned it into a supply warehouse.

I stopped the truck in the alley between the two buildings and sat in it. I looked like hell and didn't need to be out wandering around. A quick look showed side doors to both, and just beyond them, the alley became a dead end at a tall cinder-block wall that enclosed Birk's courtyard.

Once again, the only choice was to act or sit in the truck breathing carbon monoxide until it didn't matter anymore. I glanced around, saw no one, and got out. The doors were locked, but it took only a shove to open them. From the number of gouges around the battered lockset, most of the hotel staff apparently found it easier to carry a screwdriver than a key. I stepped inside.

The place smelled of mold and decay, and the drywall was spotted with water. Ceiling tiles hung swollen and broken; exposed conduit was dented and leaked insulated wire at the joints. I walked back to the truck and lifted the rifle from the gun rack, checked to make sure it was loaded, then went back inside the old hotel. I didn't bother looking around. Even if someone saw me, the odds were against their reporting me. People hate to get involved.

The stairs were no more dangerous than any other part of the dilapidated structure, and the fire doors at each level hung from their hinges. I wondered if anybody ever came in and guessed it might just be a hangout for winos and druggies. I slowed down and made my way with more caution. I didn't want to blow my one chance to get Birk by stumbling into a nest of dopers with guns. I stopped at the top floor without having seen a soul, found a room with a view of the courtyard, and settled down to wait.

When I tried to raise the window it stuck about an inch above the jamb, and, in frustration, I almost broke it out and said the hell with it. Finally, haltingly, it came loose and I bumped it up little by little until I could sit comfortably and still aim anywhere in Birk's flag-draped courtyard. It was lock-and-load time, and I slipped a shell into the chamber.

Bob Birk wasn't outside, and I was disappointed. I wanted this to be over, and I had no more patience at all. Katherine was dead and it was obscene for me to be alive. My old pal Bob and I would go together, arm in arm, wing in wing, maybe; who knows how much God can forgive? It was the longest day I had ever spent, and it didn't seem fair, now that I was in such a hurry. The general was down there, and as he kept flitting in and out of the office, I wondered if I would have the luck to nail them both. Shadows crawled under the tables and trees and snuck out the other side, and still Birk didn't show. My leg went to sleep and my shoulder woke up. I studied every window on his office building, looked at the scrubbed faces of his people. My stomach grumbled, and I knew then why Oswald brought fried chicken with him. He did it to kill time.

Somebody was shouting. I raised my chin from a cardboard box and blinked into the afternoon sun. An angry voice roared from down below and the rear door of the office crashed open. Bob Birk stepped out onto the sidewalk and pulled off his jacket, the wide expanse of white shirt an easy target. I lifted the rifle and let the stock settle on the box, steadying it with my leg and squinting down the scope.

He wasn't there. Without losing my position in the sights, I moved the end of the barrel around until I found him again. He leaned upon a loaded banquet table, but before I could squeeze off a shot he roared again and lifted his end of the table. Crystal punch bowls and cakes and flower arrangements and food raced each other to the ground, and most made it by the time he flipped the table over on its side. He yanked the wet bar down and slugged the woman bartender and probably would have done a lot of other weird things, but another woman looked up and spotted me.

In my surprise at Birk's antics I had leaned forward to get a better look and was sitting half out of the window, the rifle aimed toward the courtyard. The lady screamed and pointed, then others screamed and pointed. I ducked back into the room so fast that I forgot I was only holding the rifle in one hand. It bumped the bottom of the window and slipped from my fingers, bounced once on the ledge, and went over the side.

"Shit," I said. I groped for a handhold and tried to pull myself to my feet, but my good leg had fallen asleep, too, and I really didn't have a leg to stand on. I fell over a little pile of debris. I heard the doors downstairs crash open, heard footsteps on the stairs. I leaned back against the wall, pulled the revolver from my belt, and pointed it at the open door. A large figure dashed up the last step, and as I gripped the gun and felt for the trigger, I saw Lonnie Patrick in my sights.

"Mac!" he shouted at me, his palms out. "Don't do it!"

I was really confused, and when Lonnie plucked the pistol from my hand I just stared at him. "Birk lost the primary, Mac! It's over!"

"What?" I said as he helped me up. I stomped my disobedient foot on the floor.

"Birk never even made it to the elections, buddy." Lonnie grinned at me. "They said on the radio that it's the heaviest turnout anyone's ever seen, and he lost. He lost big!

"Let's get the hell out of here," he said, and we headed down the stairs together.

"Where's Katherine?" I said.

"In the van," Lonnie said, "with Candy. We couldn't find you, man. We've been looking everywhere!"

"Why aren't you dead?" Nobody's ever accused me of being astute. Lonnie was on the first-floor landing, and I was clomping along like mad to catch up. He shouted back at me.

"One of Willis's neighbors called him and said some guy was snooping around, asking questions—wanted to know where Willis lived," he said. "Willis called us and told us to get out of the house. We couldn't find you anywhere."

"I was out front," I said, "by the water."

"Oh, yeah?" I finally made it to the landing. "Well, you must've been doing that voodoo shit again, because we were yelling our heads off. I tell you, Mac, if you're gonna keep doing that stuff you'd better get a baby-sitter."

He pushed open the doors, and Sheriff Hall was leaning against the dead man's truck. He was pointing the huge bore of a riot gun at my chest and several of his deputies were pointing theirs our way too. Sirens wailed everywhere.

Katherine and Candy were handcuffed together and surrounded by uniforms. More and more cops raced into the alley—deputies, city cops, and troopers. All had their guns drawn.

"You fellers just hold still," Sheriff Hall said to us, and we stopped in our tracks. A deputy frisked us both and took two pistols from Lonnie, his and mine. "I believe we're about to put a stop to a whole lot of trouble, Clay. You been botherin' the good people of Palmetto Bay for a long time, but I got a feeling they won't have to worry about you anymore." He had the same smug tone Brer Fox used on Brer Rabbit.

There was a commotion in the street, and Bob Birk barged into the alley with his entourage, pushing aside deputies and policemen alike. When he saw me his eyes filled with rage. "You!" he screeched at me. "You lousy fuck! I oughta blow your fuckin' head off!"

"Oh," I said sympathetically, "have we had a bad day?"

"Goddamn!" His face turned as red as his tie, and he tore the riot gun from Sheriff Hall's hands, stepped forward, and stuck the barrel under my chin. We were practically eye-to-eye. A silver .357 Colt pistol materialized from the left, and its muzzle touched Birk's cheek.

"Drop the gun now, Mr. Birk," Willis Traxler said in a calm, conversational tone, "or I'll have to kill you."

[150]

"Stay out of this, asshole!" Birk said through his teeth, his eyes never leaving mine.

"No, sir," Willis said. "I cain't do that. Put down the gun."

"Sheriff!" Birk shouted. "This deputy was hiding these criminals in his house!"

"Traxler." Sheriff Hall was unsure, puzzled at this turn of events. "Don't make things worse, bud. Back off."

"No, sir." Willis showed respect. The end of the shotgun was buried under my chin, and it hurt like hell. Birk was sweating buckets.

"Hall!" he shouted. "Get him away from me!"

"Don't try it, sir." Willis kept cool. Without changing tempo, he raised his voice a little and said, "Drop it now, or I *will* shoot you, Mr. Birk." His voice held an intensity that surprised me. Birk pulled the shotgun from my throat and Willis took it from him. Birk stepped back, almost insane in his anger.

"Traxler." Hall stepped in front of Birk and tried to stare down Willis. "You're under arrest for insubordination. Give me your pistol, son."

"No." There was no "sir." "These is good people, Sheriff. I'm gonna make sure they leave this alley alive."

"Men," the sheriff looked around him, "if this deputy refuses to lay down his pistol again, shoot him.

"Now give me your gun."

"I cain't do that, Sheriff," Willis said. He handed the riot gun to Lonnie Patrick. "This man is a police lieutenant from Tallahassee. He's one of us." He was talking to the other cops, ignoring Sheriff Hall. "The FDLE is at the sheriff's office right now, confiscating his files." More than one uniformed man cleared his throat, and, one by one, the cops crossed to Willis Traxler's side of the alley. Hall stood with Bob Birk and three sweating deputies. The troopers and city cops stood apart from the others, studying the showdown.

"Let them women go, Carl," Willis said to a tall deputy who stood beside Katherine and Candy. "C'mon, buddy, you know what's right." The sheriff was so busy thinking, he didn't even notice this mutiny in his ranks. The two women joined Lonnie and me.

"What the hell are you talking about?" Hall said.

"Limestone Creek, Sheriff," Willis said. "It seems they's a lot of questions about what really happened that night. I thank they even gonna dig up ol' Renaldo."

"Huh?" The sheriff got smaller. Lonnie had told the people in Tallahassee that Willis was the man to work with in Palmetto Bay, and

I guess they'd done so. The other three deputies jumped ship and swam to Willis.

"The sheriff ordered me to take Renaldo there that night!" one of them told Lonnie Patrick.

"Shut up, Preston." Hall's voice was menacing.

"He ordered me to," the deputy mumbled again, sullen and scared. Birk began making puffing noises and clutched his chest. His tired-eyed daughter stepped from his group and put an arm halfway around him.

"Come on, Daddy," she said. An older man took the other side and they walked away through the hushed crowd. I looked at Katherine. She took my hands in hers and we stood touching fingers. Sheriff Hall stepped toward Birk's retreating back, then turned to his mutineers. He was a man used to power, and he didn't know what to do. He spun back to Birk again, angry.

"Birk!" he shouted, but the other man didn't stop, didn't acknowledge him. "Damn it, Birk! Your people better stand behind me on this!

"Birk!" he yelled on the move, trying to narrow the gap between them. The entourage turned the corner and vanished from sight. The cops broke into small groups and, heads together, wandered from the alley. Katherine and I missed most of it, because we were busy watching each other.

"It'll take a couple of days to close out my accounts and get my things," I said, finding it hard not to fall into those beautiful green eyes.

"I have time." She smiled. I glanced at my shoulder.

"This thing's going to take a while to heal," I said. "I'll be a burden."

"Oh, Mac." Katherine's face robbed the light from the disappearing sun. There was that smile again. "You'll always be a pain in the ass, but I love you." She moved closer.

"I want to give my house to Willis and Addie," I said. "We left their place in a mess, you know." She nodded. "I don't know how to go about it, but Mark can figure out all that, I guess."

"You'd use Mark?" Katherine asked.

"Yeah," I said, "I'd use him. He's my friend. You may not believe this, Katherine, but I don't have a lot of friends." She laughed so hard, I had to prop her up on my bruised shoulder. I decided not to tell her I was being sincere.

[152]

EPILOGUE

We had to come back to Palmetto Bay three times between Labor Day and Christmas. Candace decided to stay with Lonnie Patrick and his family in Tallahassee because of the trial and wound up getting both a place of her own and a job working in a crisis clinic. She had a hell of a résumé.

Each time we came we stayed with Torrea at the farm. She'd had a double-wide trailer moved onto the land and was attempting to put together a last edition of the *Walker's Companion*, a tribute to Mel Shiver. Her insurance company came through on the fire, and an enormous lawsuit against the government was pending. It was one of many. She told us of her plans to write a book.

The trial will never end. Not as long as lawyers live and breathe. Some of the minor players had already been found guilty by Christmas, but so far stiff fines and community service were the orders of the court. Even those were under appeal. I was paying Mr. Robert Booth Holmes on a lifetime installment plan.

I'm sure everything is still in place. It sits now, quietly waiting for another opportunity. There's an interim sheriff in the county and a new governor in the statehouse.

Mark is working his way back up, I hope.

Willis, Addie, and the kids are living in my old house. They've painted it different colors, and Addie planted flowers along the front. The neighbors think the Traxlers are wonderful. The children love the aquarium and have it filled with goldfish and black mollies.